PREJUDICE

EDITED BY DAPHNE MUSE

STORIES ABOUT HATE, IGNORANCE, REVELATION, AND TRANSFORMATION

Hyperion Books for Children
New York

 For information address Hyperion Books for Children, 114 Fifth Avenue, New York, New York 10011-5690.

First Edition
1 3 5 7 9 10 8 6 4 2

Library of Congress Cataloging-in-Publication Data

Prejudice: stories about hate, ignorance, revelation, and transformation / edited by Daphne Muse—1st ed.
p. cm.
Includes bibliographical references.
Summary: An anthology of short stories featuring young people of different backgrounds who experience prejudice.
ISBN 0-7868-0024-0 (trade)—ISBN 0-7868-1057-2 (pbk.)
1. Children's stories, American. 2. Discrimination—juvenile fiction. 3. Prejudices—Juvenile fiction. [1. Prejudices—Fiction 2. Discrimination—Fiction. 3. Short stories, American.]
I. Muse, Daphne.
PZ5.P7843 1995
[Fic]—dc20 94-35187

For Anyania and Devin

And the thousands of young people who struggle in earnest for new possibilities and justice

Contents

Acknowledgments

My thanks to Marie Brown, my agent, for connecting me with this project.

Howard Reeves, my editor at Hyperion, for his insightful questions and willingness to examine his own thinking. Bouquets of gratitude to Kristen Behrens and Joanna Johnson, both of whom attended to the myriad of details relentlessly.

I would also like to thank the staff of Mama Bears bookstore in Oakland, California, and the scores of librarians across the country who always eagerly responded to my research queries.

And from my garden of gratitude, I harvest a major thank-you for my Mills College Upward Bound Bridge students. Along with the hundreds of young people in my East Oakland community, they keep me attuned to how racism, sexism, homophobia, and classism affect the tone and tenor of young people's lives.

My heart always blossoms with gratitude for the Creative Spirit that guides and sustains me.

INTRODUCTION

Prejudice: An adverse judgment or opinion formed beforehand or without knowledge or examination of the facts. A preconceived preference or idea: bias. The act or state of holding unreasonable preconceived judgments or convictions. Irrational suspicion or hatred of a particular group, race, or religion. Detriment or injury caused to a person by the preconceived and unfavorable conviction of another or others.

—*The American Heritage Dictionary of the English Language*

Prejudice affects all of us. In classrooms, on the playground, at home, and even in places of worship, prejudice invades almost every aspect of our lives. This collection of stories invites you to go beyond your own cultural and personal borders to examine your thinking about and behavior toward people different from yourself.

As we all do, I learned prejudice from national leaders, relatives, teachers, friends, classmates, neighbors—as well as from advertising, television, and books. Each compounded a prevalent stereotype and breathed life into my own ignorance, into my own distorted ideas about people. Not until I was an adult did I discover books that helped me understand what our color, gender, or class has to do with where our families live, who our friends are, or what we learn in school.

Growing up female and "colored" in Washington, D.C., in the 1950s and '60s, I experienced the often gut-wrenching pain of racism, sexism, and classism. While within the black community my light complexion and "good" hair were hailed as an asset by some, these same people excluded me from select social circles because of my working-class roots. These attitudes negated my ability to accept myself. This kind of internalized prejudice is also reflected in the experiences of the main characters in Mavis Hara's "Carnival Queen" and Lynda Barry's "White Trash."

When I became an elementary school teacher in 1967, I made the decision not to use books that demeaned, ridiculed, or failed to acknowledge the contributions people of color had made, and continued to make, to literature, art, science, and culture. In 1968, I read *Zeely*, a young adult novel by Virginia Hamilton. This groundbreaking book celebrates the beauty of black girls and women in ways that I had never seen acknowledged before. With an ever-growing understanding, I came to see how history and conditions shaped me from a colored girl into an African American woman. I came to understand how racism, sexism, homophobia, anti-Semitism, and classism have negated the accomplishments of millions of people.

I have chosen a wide range of stories and experiences for this anthology. In Jacqueline Woodson's "Maizon at Blue Hill," an African American girl seeks to understand her place at a private boarding school, light-years away from her class and cultural background. In Jack Forbes's "Only Approved Indians Can Play: Made in USA," members of a basketball team are disqualified when they cannot prove their tribal affiliations. Chris Crutcher's "A Brief Moment in the Life of Angus Bethure" provides a forthright look at body image and prejudice against people because of their stature.

Just as books stirred my consciousness, I hope that this "family" of stories will help you to reexamine your life and how you think about and treat others. Of course, one book cannot contain all that there is to be said about prejudice. The quest for some of the best stories made it possible for me to revisit the works of well-known writers. I also had the opportunity to read the works of those whose voices are not as familiar. But I was dismayed by the dearth of contemporary novels and short stories for young adults that deal with prejudice and the ability to transform our lives beyond its constricting and suffocating paralysis. In addition to the many more stories that need to be written, shared, and discussed, I hope those collected here will help you in joining, or continuing your support of, the struggle to create a just and equitable society.

White Trash

from The Good Times Are Killing Me

Lynda Barry

Have you ever met white trash before? The kind that listens to white trash music? The first white trash I ever met was Ranette Bosems who came to our school new in the middle of the year. You could have thought she would be popular at first because she had the longest hair of anyone we had ever seen. Then you noticed the ugly clothes and by third recess you noticed that she was pretty easy to make fun of. It started with her name but it could have started with anything, any part of her. Her last name wasn't really Bosems but that is how our teacher said it at first by accident and when we all started laughing, Ranette said her real name loud and the teacher said, "I'm sorry," but it was too late and that is what we called her and if I saw her today that is all I would know to call her because no one remembered her real name after that. Another thing about her was she talked funny and I couldn't figure out what she even was until Bonna called her white trash when she stared at Bonna doing her turns on the monkey bars. Then Ranette said it. She said The Word. She called Bonna a nigger. I remember it felt like the whole recess just stopped like in a science fiction movie where someone presses a button and everyone gets frozen except for two people. I have to say I felt kind of sorry for Ranette right then. She was stupid to have said The Word. I never said The Word, even when I was alone. Bonna popped off that monkey bar and was standing in front of Ranette faster than I could see her move.

"What'd you just call me, girl?" Bonna said. Deborah Small and Gina Davenport went and stood by Bonna, but nobody came to stand by Ranette. We all just watched. "Huh hillbilly white girl? What'd you just say to me? Say it again. Say it again so I can kick your ass," and that's when Mrs. Vidrine came and asked what was going on here. Bonna told her Ranette had called her a nigger and Mrs. Vidrine grabbed Ranette's arm and said, "Now you listen to me.

"We don't use those words here you understand? You leave those words back where you came from," she said. "They don't have any place here. I don't want to hear that word come out of your mouth again." And she dragged both Ranette and Bonna to the office because the school rules were, no matter who started it, you both get in trouble.

Nobody would ever stand by Ranette. Ranette's germs, no returns. I felt sorry for her in a way because she couldn't help it if she was a hillbilly. Whenever she walked by, Bonna called her "white trash." "Want to see what some white trash looks like?" she'd say. "Go look in the mirror."

About a week after Ranette first came, our teacher sent her out of the room with a note to go get something and when Ranette left, our teacher said, "Class, I have something important I want to talk to you about." And then she told us she didn't like the way we were treating Ranette.

"Just because she is different than the rest of you is no reason to be mean to her." Bonna raised her hand and told how Ranette had called her a nigger to her face.

"She just made a mistake, Bonna," our teacher said. "Where she comes from, people still use words like that. She didn't know any better. She didn't know that we don't say those things here. She has a lot of things to learn but she won't be able to unless all of us help her and are willing to be friends with her." And then our teacher did something that meant that Ranette would be off-limits to us for the rest of her life. She assigned her a special friend of the week. The special friend had to play with Ranette during every recess for one week and sit by her at lunch. First she asked people to volunteer and nobody raised their hands. Then she picked me.

Ranette didn't live all that far from us, just down

Crowley behind the lumberyard in those houses my cousin Ellen called the boondocks after a song she knew. There wasn't even a street down there by those houses, just mud roads. When Ranette said would I come over, I was thinking that maybe if I went I would get some extra credit points plus I could tell Bonna all about what the inside of the white trashes' houses looked like.

You know how Ranette talks funny? Well her mom and dad I couldn't even understand. Accents was the problem. I felt sorry for them getting stuck talking like that for the rest of their lives. Compared to them, everyone I knew was lucky.

Ranette came from down where it was popular to want slaves. Our teacher told us that the people there are backwards people. I looked around at Ranette's house and thought so these are them. The Backwards People. Her mother was in the kitchen listening to backwards music coming out of the radio. That kind of music could be OK if everybody didn't already know that only stupid people listened to it. That it is prejudiced music and if you got it playing in your house you are stupid and prejudiced too. My cousin Ellen would get embarrassed if she even just accidentally hit that radio station when she was moving the dialer around. And here at poor Ranette's house they didn't just have that station on, they had it blasting on, louder than we ever played anything at our house.

Ranette showed me to her mom whose hair was in pin

curlers and who I couldn't really understand except she embarrassed me by being so nice and saying something like what a pleasure that I came over and did I want something to eat. Once Ranette was in her house she didn't look so full of germs all of a sudden, and we sat down at their table and ate yellow bread that had the most crumbs of any bread I ever saw and drank milk out of blue metal glasses while Mrs. Bosems combed out Ranette's hair and braided it and laughed whenever I had to ask Ranette what she was saying to me. The part that I didn't get was how come Mrs. Bosems could understand me perfect?

After my week of being her special friend it turns out I ended up being real friends with Ranette and I went to her house a lot, but I made her swear to God not to tell on me for it. I felt bad in a way about making her keep it a secret but there was nothing I could do. Was it supposed to be my fault that they had been stupid enough to want slaves? That they had to go and mess up America for everybody?

Our teacher told us that every Negro in the class had come from slaves and that everybody else was probably related to someone who had owned them. That afternoon we had some big fights on the play field. It was the first time I ever got shoved in the bathroom for no reason.

My father said that they should just get some money together and just send all of the Negroes back to Africa. Everyone agrees it was a mistake to bring them here in the first place and they aren't happy, so why can't we just send them back to where they will be happy. I asked Bonna if she wanted to go back to Africa and she said the only place she wanted to go back to was Washington, D.C.

Ranette didn't come to school for a whole week and so finally when no one was looking I walked down to her house to see if she was sick. When I turned the corner I saw their door standing wide open and when I came up the stairs I could see that the whole house was empty except for some cardboard boxes and garbage on the floor. I wondered for a while if they all got kidnapped and then I figured no, that's not what happened.

I walked through all the rooms and then I walked into Ranette's. I could smell the smell of her. On the windowsill I saw one of her hair fasteners and I put it in my pocket. I stood for a long time with my forehead on her window, digging my fingernails into her hair fastener and just staring at everything she ever stared at.

On the floor of their kitchen I found a pencil and I wrote my whole name in cursive on the inside of one drawer. And if I ever see Ranette again all I can think of is that I am going to sock her in the stomach.

from Chernowitz!

Fran Arrick

It was bad, waking up every morning with a soggy cloud hanging over your day. Spring had come, which always made me feel so good before. Now I hated it, because nobody was so intent on hurrying into buses and buildings any more, or huddling inside his own jacket or his own space. Now the kids moved around, stayed out longer, felt freer and acted that way. Before, when I'd get to the bus stop just in time to walk on the bus, the kids would be clustered together, shivering, and looking up and down the road for the bus's arrival. When the warm weather came, they spread out. Some of them were way up my road, ready to meet me coming down. They didn't touch me, but they'd fall in right behind me, and I mean *right* behind, dogging my footsteps, kicking my shoes with theirs while they walked and snickering when Emmett and Brian would say things like "C.K.C.—C.K.C." in a chant. It meant "Christ-killer Cherno," which Sundback let me know up front, so they could chant it out loud without anyone else understanding it. Then they'd chant it on the bus, like a school cheer, so that even the seventh and eighth graders picked it up, giggling, not knowing what it meant, but feeling big-shot. After a while the bus driver would shut them up, but they'd made their point and I'd hear "C.K.C." all over school.

I still managed to keep my grades up in everything except English, my best subject, but that was because I was afraid to open my mouth any more and my class-participation grade dropped like a stone. Mr. Shafer spoke to me about it a few times and each time I just said I'd try to do better but I didn't and he quit talking to me when all I did was clam up. I felt bad because I knew he was really trying, but I still wasn't about to say anything to him.

It got even worse when my mother told me that Mrs. Denny had called Mrs. Kuhn about a car pool to soccer and then Mrs. Kuhn called Mom and they worked it out that the three of them would drive back and forth.

"So now I have to ride with Brian and Tim both?" I asked, feeling like my stomach was a lead ball. "I didn't even know Mrs. Denny knew Mrs. Kuhn." The Kuhns live two back roads up from the lake.

"Well, she didn't, but she found out that there was

another kid on your team from the lake area and decided it was silly not to take advantage of it. Milly Kuhn called me because *she* thought it was silly, too. After all, there are three of us and with everyone's time limited, not to mention gas prices—"

I turned away. I had to lean on the table. I felt dizzy.

"Oh, come on now, Bobby, it's only a ride, back and forth from the Oronco Pond field twice a week. Now maybe you don't like these boys any more, but can't you live with that to save me a little extra time and money?"

They hate Jews, Ma, can you live with *that*? But I only said it in my head.

I could quit soccer, I figured. But I really didn't want to and besides, how could I explain it.

All right, what could happen with somebody's mother right in the front seat all the time?

"Okay," I said finally. "Okay, okay."

"Bobby, you know, you could make an effort to get along with these boys. You were once such good friends, why, you and Timmy Kuhn were in nursery school together, you've been all through grade school together. Whatever happened to change your attitude like that?"

I shook my head helplessly. That was when I came closest to telling her, but I knew it was *my* problem and *my* responsibility. My parents deal with the community all the time. How would they feel, knowing . . . knowing . . .

Absolutely not. I wouldn't say anything unless something happened that affected them. And nothing had and I felt sure nothing would, either. I'd gotten the feeling that Sundback wanted no problems with adults; nothing he'd ever done to me was in the presence of an adult. And I remembered Halloween, which I was sure would have been much worse if my father hadn't been outside the whole time.

The rides to practice were bad but bearable. Brian and Tim would sit bunched together and talk only to each other, usually in whispers. When my mother drove, I'd sit in front and stare straight ahead. It just killed me when my mother would be so friendly to them.

She'd say, "Well, how's school, Brian? Your mother tells me you're a real math whiz!" Or, "We haven't seen you at the house in so long, Tim, why don't you stop over sometime soon?"

Then one would nudge the other and grin or wink and say, "Oh, yeah, Mrs. Cherno, school's fine" and "Yeah, I'll come over real soon!" And then I'd have to hear it later about why didn't I make an effort to join the conversation?

At last—school ended.

I really welcomed exam week because everybody was too busy studying to pay much attention to me, all except for Sundback and his cousin, who probably didn't study at all. I hoped they both failed everything because in the fall I'd be in tenth grade and they'd still be in junior high—I'd never have to see them again for a whole year. Except on the bus . . .

I could tell that Sundback wanted me to cheat for him again in English, just by the way he kept trying to get my attention when we sat down. But I ignored him and the test was all essay anyway, so there wasn't much either of us could do about it even if I wanted to.

My overall average was ninety-two. Three points down from what it was in eighth grade. My parents could hardly complain about a ninety-two, but they muttered about the drop in points and my "attitude," which was becoming my mother's favorite word.

The soccer season ended with us finishing third, but I'd really lost interest in it after the first couple of weeks. I thought if I played real well, it would be a way of maybe winning back Brian and Tim Kuhn, but even when I played fantastically it didn't work and after a while I stopped caring what they thought. It was all an act. They put one on for Sundback and then on the soccer field they put on one for their parents. But I did, too . . . So did I.

When the Mets didn't get any better, I decided that all the bad things in the world were happening to me, but that was okay because while other people spread out their troubles, I was getting all mine over with in one year and it would be smooth sailing from then on.

Right? . . .

We have a Sunfish. It's a little sailboat. My father bought it from the people who used to live in the Dennys' house, before they moved away. I guess they could have sold it to the Dennys but we were friends and we asked them when their house first went on the market. I used to take sailing lessons from a college kid who grew up on the lake and I enjoyed going out on it. Our association ran Sunfish races every weekend: Saturdays were for the "Juniors," the kids, and Sundays for the grownups. I never entered the races. Maybe that's another thing about me that wasn't "one of the boys," but I simply wasn't interested in the boat as a competitive thing. I just liked the feeling of skimming across the water, seeming to go much faster than you actually are, watching the tiny waves lick up the side of the boat, feeling like an extension of water, wind and sky. Competition—races—they were okay if that's what you liked, it just wasn't *my* thing.

The summer before ninth grade, I entered some races with Brian because he wanted to. You're supposed to race with two, pilot and crew, and he and I took turns sailing and being the crew after I taught him how. We came in second once, the closest we ever came to winning. He was really hot on winning and I really wasn't, but I tried, to accommodate him. He didn't get how I felt about the boat but I understood how he felt about winning, so I worked at it for him. When the season ended, he said, "Next year we'll show 'em, Bobby, next year we'll sail the course during the week and practice and by the weekends we ought to be great!" I'd said, "Sure, we'll do that," figuring I'd still have lots of time for private sailing. It didn't hurt me to do the races, I just didn't think it was the point of having the boat.

This past summer, after my Sundback Year, I thought I'd have all the time I wanted for private sailing, but Denny's lack of loyalty faked me out again.

Right before the July Fourth weekend, Sundback went with his mother and his sister to visit relatives in Minnesota. I found that out when there was no motorcycle noise and no gang hanging around the dam. My mother remarked about the peace and quiet to some neighbor in the supermarket and that's what the neighbor told her. And with Sundback gone, the other kids just went on doing what they always did, swimming at the beach or playing tennis or whatever.

I went to the beach, too. It was a little private beach for the lake association families so it was never very crowded except on weekends, when the families brought their company and all their kids.

When I went down I'd see the people I always saw plus the summer people who rented houses on the lake every year. If Kuhn or Neimeier or Gustafson or any of those guys were around they left me alone; they didn't try the bus stop stuff on me and they didn't chant or anything or dunk me in the water. I was alone, but I didn't mind. It was a lot better than being picked on.

And I worked, too. I cut lawns. I took care of five lawns—including my own, which I didn't get paid for—

and my customers kept me pretty busy. So I used sailing as my little reward when I was through work for the day.

We keep the boat right at our own dock in the back of our house. One day in July, while Sundback was still gone, I went down, rigged the sail, and went out. It was a calm day, no wind, but it was nice. I had on a swimsuit and figured I'd just get a tan, like the one I had in Florida.

The idea of a tan made me think of Matty Greeley, whom I hadn't said a word to besides "Hi" the rest of the school year. Once it had looked as if she were stopping to say more to me but I didn't give her a chance, I just took off. All I could see was Sundback making a fool of me when I looked at Matty. But then, in the boat, I thought about calling her up. With Sundback gone and no school—

The sound of my name cut through my thoughts. I looked up. Brian Denny was floating by my boat on an inflated truck tire inner tube.

"Hey," he said. "How you doing?"

I couldn't believe it. That was really chutzpah! I didn't answer him and started to tack, but he paddled with his hands and caught up easily, since I needed a breeze to move and he didn't.

"You want to enter the Saturday race?" he asked, as if nothing at all had happened all year. I just stared at him.

"Hey, I said you wanna race Saturday?" he repeated, paddling all around my boat.

"What's the matter, can't you go with any of your friends?" I asked.

He didn't answer that and then I almost smiled as I remembered that Tim Kuhn always raced with Cliff Neimeier—they'd been together for years. And Gustafson and Levoy didn't sail. The other kids were either younger or older and he didn't know them that well anyway. So if Denny wanted to go sailing he'd either have to buy his own boat or use mine. That's why he was coming on.

"Denny," I said, "you're either short on brains or you've got nerve in your veins instead of blood. Paddle the hell out of here."

"Ah, come on, Cherno, can't you take a joke or anything? That's why you have such a bad time, you're so goddam serious. Neimeier says you were always like that."

He has nobody to hang around with and he can't stand it, I thought. Or he wants to sail worse than anything.

I leaned over and stared at him. "Calling somebody a Jew-bastard is a joke to you?" I said.

"Come on, it's just a word, it doesn't mean anything," he said with a wave of his fingers.

I started to go.

"It didn't mean anything!" he repeated. "What was I gonna call you, 'Mr. Too-Serious'? We were only teasing you . . ."

I didn't sail away from him but I tuned him out. Part of me wanted to say okay to him. Even though I'd never forget what he did, he obviously could. Maybe it really didn't mean something so ominous to him, even though it was ominous. And evil. But if I was the only one who thought so . . .

And if I made friends with him, then at least when he knew how I felt he'd never let something like that happen again . . .

I stared at the water. Brian had hurt me more than I even realized. I was thinking how much fun we'd had before, how convenient it was to have a friend living so close, how many fun things there were to do with someone else all summer . . . Overlooking not only how quickly he'd dropped me, but the horrible things he'd said, just to be a part of the gang.

Calling someone a name probably didn't have significance for him. He'd just go along with whatever the kids did, just so they'd like him. And now there were no kids around, only me. That was Brian Denny. My friend.

"What do you say, Bobby, you wanna forget it?" he was saying as his tube bobbed up and down in the water.

"I can't forget it, Brian," I said quietly, but I still didn't sail the boat away.

After a minute, he slid off the tube and started swimming with it toward his house.

Only Approved Indians Can Play: Made in USA

Jack Forbes

The all-Indian basketball tournament was in its second day. Excitement was pretty high, because a lot of the teams were very good or at least eager and hungry to win. Quite a few people had come to watch, mostly Indians. Many were relatives or friends of the players. A lot of people were betting money and tension was pretty great.

A team from the Tucson Inter-Tribal House was set to play against a group from the Great Lakes region. The Tucson players were mostly very dark young men with long black hair. A few had little goatee beards or mustaches though, and one of the Great Lakes fans had started a rumor that they were really Chicanos. This was a big issue since the Indian Sports League had a rule that all the players had to be of one-quarter or more Indian blood and that they had to have their BIA[1] roll numbers available if challenged.

And so a big argument started. One of the biggest, darkest Indians on the Tucson team had been singled out as a Chicano, and the crowd wanted him thrown out. The Great Lakes players, most of whom were pretty light, refused to start. They all had their BIA identification cards, encased in plastic. This proved that they were all Indians, even a blonde-haired guy. He was really only about one-sixteenth but the BIA rolls had been changed for his tribe so legally he was one-fourth. There was no question about the Great Lakes team. They were all land-based, federally recognized Indians, although living in a big midwestern city, and they had their cards to prove it.

Anyway, the big, dark Tucson Indian turned out to be a Papago. He didn't have a BIA card but he could talk Papago so they let him alone for the time being. Then they turned towards a lean, very Indian-looking guy who had a pretty big goatee. He seemed to have a Spanish accent, so they demanded to see his card.

Well, he didn't have one either. He said he was full-blood Tarahumara Indian and he could also speak his language.

[1] Bureau of Indian Affairs

None of the Great Lakes Indians could talk their languages so they said that was no proof of anything, that you had to have a BIA roll number.

The Tarahumara man was getting pretty angry by then. He said his father and uncle had been killed by the whites in Mexico and that he did not expect to be treated with prejudice by other Indians.

But all that did no good. Someone demanded to know if he had a reservation and if his tribe was recognized. He replied that his people lived high up in the mountains and that they were still resisting the Mexicanos, that the government was trying to steal their land.

"What state do your people live in," they wanted to know. When he said that his people lived free, outside of the control of any state, they only shook their fists at him. "You're not an official Indian. All official Indians are under the whiteman's rule now. We all have a number given to us, to show that we are recognized."

Well, it all came to an end when someone shouted that "Tarahumaras don't exist. They're not listed in the BIA dictionary." Another fan yelled, "He's a Mexican. He can't play. This tournament is only for Indians."

The officials of the tournament had been huddling together. One blew his whistle and an announcement was made. "The Tucson team is disqualified. One of its members is a Yaqui. One is a Tarahumara. The rest are Papagos. None of them have BIA enrollment cards. They are not

Indians within the meaning of the laws of the government of the United States. The Great Lakes team is declared the winner by default."

A tremendous roar of applause swept through the stands. A white BIA official wiped the tears from his eyes and said to a companion, "God Bless America. I think we've won."

Carnival Queen

Mavis Hara

My friend Terry and I both have boy's nicknames. But that's the only thing about us that is the same. Terry is beautiful. She is about 5′4″ tall, which is tall enough to be a stewardess. I am only 5 feet tall, which is too short, so I should know.

My mother keeps asking me why Terry is my friend. This makes me nervous, because I really don't know. Ever since we had the first senior class officers' meeting at my house and my mother found the empty Tampax container in our wastebasket she has been really asking a lot of questions about Terry. Terry and I are the only girls who were elected to office. She's treasurer and I'm secretary. The president, the vice-president, and the sergeant-at-arms are all boys. I guess that's why Terry and I hang out together. Like when we have to go to class activities and meetings she picks me up. I never even knew her before we were elected. I don't know who she used to hang around with, but it sure wasn't me and my friends. We're too, Japanese girl, you know, plain. I mean, Terry has skin like a porcelain doll. She has cheekbones like Garbo, body like Ann-Margret, she has legs like, well, like not any Japanese girl I've ever seen. Like I said, she's beautiful. She always dresses perfectly, too. She always wears an outfit, a dress with matching straw bag and colored leather shoes. Her hair is always set, combed, and sprayed, she even wears nylon stockings under her jeans, even on really hot days. Terry is the only girl I know who has her own Liberty House charge card. Not that she ever goes shopping by herself. Whenever she goes near a store, her mother goes with her.

Funny, Terry has this beautiful face, perfect body, and nobody hates her. We hate Valerie Rosecrest. Valerie is the only girl in our P.E. class who can come out of the girls' showers, wrap a towel around herself under her arms and have it stay up by itself. No hands. She always takes the longest time in the showers and walks back to her locker past the rest of us, who are already dry and fumbling with the one hook on the back of our bras. Valerie's bra has five hooks on the back of it and needs all of them to stay closed. I think she hangs that thing across the top of her locker door on purpose just so we can walk past it and be blinded by it shining in the afternoon sun. One time, my friend Tina got fed up and snatched Val's bra. She wore it on top of her head and ran around the locker room. I swear, she looked like an albino Mickey Mouse. Nobody did anything but laugh. Funny, it was Terry who took the bra away and put it back on Val's locker again.

I don't know why we're friends, but I wasn't surprised when we ended up together as contestants in the Carnival Queen contest. The Carnival Queen contest is a tradition at McKinley. They have pictures of every Carnival Queen ever chosen hanging in the auditorium corridor right next to the pictures of the senators, governors, politicians, and millionaires who graduated from the school. This year there are already five portraits of queens up there. All the girls are wearing long ball gowns and the same rhinestone crown which is placed on their heads by Mr. Harano, the principal. They have elbow length white gloves and they're carrying baby's breath and roses. The thing is, all the girls are hapa.[1] Every one.

Every year, it is the same tradition. A big bunch of girls gets nominated to run, but everybody knows from intermediate school on which girl in the class is actually going to win. She has to be hapa.

"They had to nominate me," I try to tell Terry. "I'm a class officer, but you, you actually have a chance to be the only Japanese girl to win." Terry had just won the

[1] from the Hawaiian *hapa haole*, someone of part-white ancestry or origin

American Legion essay contest the week before. You would think that being fashionable and coordinated all the time would take all her energy and wear her out, but her mother wants her to be smart too. She looks at me with this sad face I don't understand.

"I doubt it," she says.

Our first orientation meeting for contestants is today in the library after school. I walk to the meeting actually glad to be there after class. The last after school meeting I went to was the one I was forced to attend. That one had no contestants. Just potential school dropouts. The first meeting, I didn't know anybody there. Nobody I know in the student government crowd is like me and has actually flunked chemistry. All the guys who were coming in the door were the ones who hang around the bathrooms that I'm too scared to use. Nobody ever threatened me though, and after a while, dropout class wasn't half bad, but I have to admit, I like this meeting better. I sit down and watch the other contestants come through the door. I know the first name of almost every girl who walks in. Terry, of course, who is wearing her blue suede jumper and silk blouse, navy stockings and navy patent leather shoes. My friend Trudye, who has a great figure for an Oriental girl but who wears braces and Coke bottle glasses. My friend Linda, who has a beautiful face but a basic musubi-shaped[2] body. The Yanagawa twins, who

[2] literally, shaped like a rice ball

have beautiful hapa faces, but pretty tragic, they inherited their father's genes and have government-issue Japanese-girl legs. Songleaders, cheerleaders, ROTC[3] sponsors, student government committee heads, I know them all. Krissie Clifford, who is small and blond, comes running in late. Krissie looks like a young version of Beaver's mother on the TV show. She's always running like she just fell out of the screen, and if she moves fast enough, she can catch up with the TV world and jump back in. Then she walks in. Leilani Jones. As soon as she walks in the door, everybody in the room turns to look at her. Everybody in the room knows that Leilani is the only girl who can possibly win.

Lani is hapa, Japanese-haole. She inherited the best features from everybody. She is tall and slim, with light brown hair and butter frosting skin. I don't even know what she is wearing. Leilani is so beautiful it doesn't matter what she is wearing. She is smooth, and gracefully quiet. Her smile is soft and shiny. It's like looking at a pearl. Lani is not only beautiful, when you look at her all you hear is silence, like the air around her is stunned. We all know it. This is the only girl who can possibly win.

As soon as Leilani walks in, Mrs. Takahara, the teacher advisor, says, "Well, now, take your seats everyone. We can begin."

We each take a wooden chair on either side of two rows

[3] Reserve Officer Training Candidate

of long library tables. There is a make-up kit and mirror at each of the places. Some of Mrs. Takahara's friends who are teachers are also sitting in.

"This is Mrs. Chung, beauty consultant of Kamedo cosmetics," Mrs. Takahara says. "She will show us the proper routines of skin cleansing and make-up. The Carnival Queen contest is a very special event. All the girls who are contestants must be worthy representatives of McKinley High School. This means the proper make-up and attitude. Mrs. Chung . . ."

I have to admire the beauty consultant. Even though her make-up is obvious as scaffolding in front of a building, it is so well done, kinda like the men who dance the girls' parts in Kabuki[4] shows, you look at it and actually believe that what you are seeing is her face.

"First, we start with proper cleansing," she says. We stare into our own separate mirrors.

"First, we pin our hair so that it no longer hangs in our faces." All of the girls dig in handbags and come up with bobby pins. Hairstyles disappear as we pin our hair straight back. The teachers look funny, kind of young without their teased hair. Mrs. Chung walks around to each station. She squeezes a glop of pink liquid on a cotton ball for each of us.

"Clean all the skin well," she says. "Get all the dirt and impurities out." We scrub hard with that cotton ball, we all

[4] Japanese traditional drama in which all parts are played by men

know that our skin is loaded with lots of stuff that is impure. My friend Trudye gets kinda carried away. She was scrubbing so hard around her eyes that she scrubbed off her Scotch tape. She hurries over to Mrs. Takahara's chair, mumbles something and excuses herself. I figure she'll be gone pretty long; the only bathroom that is safe for us to use is all the way over in the other building.

"Now we moisturize," Mrs. Chung is going on. "We use this step to correct defects in the tones of our skins." I look over at Terry. I can't see any defects in any of the tones of her skin.

"This mauve moisturizer corrects sallow undertones," Mrs. Chung says.

"What's shallow?" I whisper to Terry.

"SALLOW," she whispers back disgusted. "Yellow."

"Oh," I say and gratefully receive the large glop of purple stuff Mrs. Chung is squeezing on my new cotton ball. Mrs. Chung squeezes a little on Terry's cotton ball too. When she passes Lani, she smiles and squeezes white stuff out from a different tube.

I happily sponge the purple stuff on. Terry is sponging too but I notice she is beginning to look like she has the flu. "Next, foundation," says Mrs. Chung. She is walking around, narrowing her eyes at each of us and handing us each a tube that she is sure is the correct color to bring out the best in our skin. Mrs. Chung hands me a plastic tube of dark beige. She gives Terry a tube of lighter beige and gives Lani a different tube altogether.

"Just a little translucent creme," she smiles to Lani who smiles back rainbow bubbles and strands of pearls.

Trudye comes rushing back and Linda catches her up on all the steps she's missed. I gotta admit, without her glasses and with all that running, she has really pretty cheekbones and nice colored skin. I notice she has new Scotch tape on too, and is really concentrating on what Mrs. Chung is saying next.

"Now that we have the proper foundation, we concentrate on the eyes." She pulls out a rubber and chrome pincer machine. She stands in front of Linda with it. I become concerned.

"The eyelashes sometimes grow in the wrong direction," Mrs. Chung informs us. "They must be trained to bend correctly. We use the Eyelash Curler to do this." She hands the machine to Linda. I watch as Linda puts the metal pincer up to her eye and catches her straight, heavy black lashes between the rubber pincer blades.

"Must be sore if they do it wrong and squeeze the eyelid meat," I breathe to Terry. Terry says nothing. She looks upset, like she is trying not to bring up her lunch.

"Eyeshadow must be applied to give the illusion of depth," says Mrs. Chung. "Light on top of the lid, close to the lashes, luminescent color on the whole lid, a dot of white in the center of the iris, and brown below the browbone to accentuate the crease." Mrs. Chung is going pretty fast now. I wonder what the girls who have Oriental eyelids without a crease are going to do. I check out the room quickly, over the top of my make-up mirror. Sure enough, all the Oriental girls here have a nice crease in their lids. Those who don't are wearing Scotch tape. Mrs. Chung is passing out "pearlescent" eyeshadow.

"It's made of fish scales," Terry says. I have eyelids that are all right, but eyeshadow, especially sparking eyeshadow, makes me look like a gecko, you know, with protruding eye sockets that go in separate directions. Terry has beautiful deep-socketed eyes and browbones that don't need any help to look well defined. I put on the stuff in spite of my better judgment and spend the rest of the time trying not to move my eyeballs too much, just in case anybody notices. Lani is putting on all this make-up too. But in her case, it just increases the pearly glow that her skin is already producing.

"This ends the make-up session," Mrs. Chung is saying. "Now our eyes and skins have the proper preparation for our roles as contestants for Carnival Queen."

"Ma, I running in the Carnival Queen contest," I was saying last night. My mother got that exasperated look on her face.

"You think you get chance!"

"No, but the teachers put in the names of all the student council guys." My mother is beginning to look like she is suffering again.

"When you were small, everybody used to tell me you should run for Cherry Blossom contest. But that was before you got so dark like your father. I always tell you no go out in the sun or wear lotion like me when you go out but you never listen."

"Yeah, Ma, but we get modeling lessons, make-up, how to walk."

"Good, might make you stand up straight. I would get you a back brace, but when you were small, we paid so much money for your legs, to get special shoes connected to a bar. You only cried and never would wear them. That's why you still have crooked legs."

That was last night. Now I'm here and Mrs. Takahara is telling us about the walking and modeling lessons.

"Imagine a string coming out of the top of your skull and connected to the ceiling. Shorten the string and walk with your chin out and back erect. Float! Put one foot in front of the other, point your toes outward and glide forward on the balls of your feet. When you stop, place one foot slightly behind the other at a forty-five degree angle. Put your weight on the back foot . . ." I should have worn the stupid shoes when I was small. I'm bow-legged. Just like my father. Leilani is not bow-legged. She looks great putting one long straight tibia in front of the other. I look kinda like a crab. We walk in circles around and around the room. Terry is definitely not happy. She's walking pretty far away from me. Once, when I pass her, I could swear she is crying.

"Wow, long practice, yeah?" I say as we walk across the lawn heading toward the bus. Terry, Trudye, Linda, and I are still together. A black Buick pulls up to the curb.

Terry’s Mom has come to pick her up. Terry’s Mom always picks her up. She must have just come back from the beauty shop. Her head is wrapped in a pink net wind bonnet. Kind of like the cake we always get at weddings that my mother keeps on top of the television and never lets anybody eat.

“I’ll call you,” Terry says.

‘“I’m so glad that you and Theresa do things together,” Terry’s mother says. “Theresa needs girlfriends like you, Sam.” I’m looking at the pink net around her face. I wonder if Terry’s father ever gets the urge to smash her hair down to feel the shape of her head. Terry looks really uncomfortable as they drive away.

I feel uncomfortable too. Trudye and Linda’s make-up looks really weird in the afternoon sunlight. My eyeballs feel larger than tank turrets and they must be glittering brilliantly too. The Liliha Puunui bus comes and we all get on. The long center aisle of the bus gives me an idea. I put one foot in front of the other and practice walking down. Good thing it is late and the guys we go to school with are not getting on.

“You think Leilani is going to win?” Trudye asks.

“What?” I say as I almost lose my teeth against the metal pole I’m holding on to. The driver has just started up, and standing with your feet at a forty-five degree angle doesn’t work on public transportation.

“Lani is probably going to win, yeah?” Trudye says again. She can hide her eye make-up behind her glasses and looks pretty much OK. "I'm going to stay in for the experience. Plus, I'm going to the orthodontist and take my braces out, and I asked my mother if I could have contact lenses and she said OK." Trudye goes on, but I don't listen. I get a seat by the window and spend the whole trip looking out so nobody sees my fish-scale eyes.

I am not surprised when I get home and the phone begins to ring.

"Sam, it's Terry. You stay in the contest. But I decided I'm not going to run."

"That's nuts, Terry," I am half screaming at her, "you are the only one of us besides Lani that has a chance to win. You could be the first Japanese Carnival Queen that McKinley ever has." I am going to argue this one.

"Do you know the real name of this contest?" Terry asks.

"I don't know, Carnival Queen. I've never thought about it I guess."

"It's Carnival Queen Scholarship Contest."

"Oh, so?" I'm still interested in arguing that only someone with legs like Terry even has a chance.

"Why are you running? How did you get nominated?" Terry asks.

"I'm Senior Class secretary, they had to nominate me, but you . . ."

"And WHY are you secretary," she cuts me off before I get another running start about chances.

"I don't know, I guess because I used to write poems for

English class and they always got in the paper of the yearbook. And probably because Miss Chuck made me write a column for the newspaper for one year to bring up my social studies grade."

"See . . . and why am I running?"

"OK, you're class officer, and sponsor, and you won the American Legion essay contest . . ."

"And Krissy?"

"She's editor of the yearbook, and a sponsor, and the Yanagawa twins are songleaders and Trudye is prom committee chairman and Linda . . ." I am getting into it.

"And Lani," says Terry quietly.

"Well, she's a sponsor I think . . ." I've lost some momentum. I really don't know.

"I'm a sponsor, and I know she's not," Terry says.

"Student government? No . . . I don't think so . . . not cheering, her sister is the one in the honor society, not . . . hey, no, couldn't be . . ."

"That's right," Terry says, "the only reason she's running is because she's supposed to win." It couldn't be true. "That means the rest of us are all running for nothing. The best we can do is second place." My ears are getting sore with the sense of what she says. "We're running because of what we did. But we're going to lose because of what we look like. Look, it's still good experience and you can still run if you like."

"Nah . . . ," I say, still dazed by it. "But what about Mrs. Takahara, what about your mother?" Terry is quiet.

"I think I can handle Mrs. Takahara," Terry finally says.

"I'll say I'm not running, too. If it's two of us, it won't be so bad." I am actually kind of relieved that this is the last day I'll have to put gecko eye make-up all over my face.

"Thanks, Sam . . . ," Terry says.

"Yeah . . . my mother will actually be relieved. Ever since I forgot the ending at my piano recital in fifth grade, she gets really nervous if I'm in front of any audience."

"You want me to pick you up for the Carnival Saturday night?" Terry asks.

"I'll ask my Mom," I say. "See you then . . ."

"Yeah . . ."

I think, "We're going to lose because of what we look like." I need a shower, my eyes are itching anyway. I'm glad my mother isn't home yet. I think best in the shower and sometimes I'm in there an hour or more.

Soon, with the world a small square of warm steam and tile walls, it all starts going through my head. The teachers looked so young in the make-up demonstration with their hair pinned back—they looked kind of like us. But we are going to lose because of what we look like. I soap the layers of make-up off my face. I guess they're tired of looking like us; musubi bodies, daikon[5] legs, furoshiki-shaped[6], home-made dresses, bento[7] tins to be packed in the early

[5] a Japanese white radish; unlike red radishes, daikons are long and thin

[6] a square scarflike cloth used to wrap things in

[7] box lunch; lunch box

mornings, mud and sweat everywhere. The water is splashing down on my face and hair. But Krissy doesn't look like us, and she is going to lose too. Krissy looks like the Red Cross society lady from intermediate school. She looks like Beaver's mother on the television show. Too haole. She's going to lose because of the way she looks. Lani doesn't look anything like anything from the past. She looks like something that could only have been born underwater where all motions are slow and all sounds are soft. I turn off the water and towel off. Showers always make me feel clean and secure. I guess I can't blame even the teachers, everyone wants to feel safe and secure.

My mother is sitting at the table peeling an orange. She does this almost every night and I already know what she's going to say.

"Eat this orange, good for you, lots of vitamin C."

"I don't want to eat orange now, Ma." I know it is useless, but I say it anyway. My mother is the kind of Japanese lady who will hunch down real small when she passes in front of you when you're watching TV. Makes you think she's quiet and easygoing, but not on the subject of vitamin C.

"I peeled it already. Want it." Some people actually think that my mother is shy.

"I not running in the contest. Terry and I going quit."

"Why?" my mother asks, like she really doesn't need to know.

"Terry said that we running for nothing. Everybody

already knows Lani going win." My mother looks like she just tasted some orange peel.

"That's not the real reason." She hands me the orange and starts washing the dishes.

There's lots of things I don't understand. Like why Terry hangs out with me. Why my mother is always so curious about her and now why she doesn't think this is the real reason that Terry is quitting the contest.

"What did the mother say about Terry quitting the contest?" my mother asks without turning around.

"I donno, nothing I guess."

"Hmmmmmm . . . that's not the real reason. That girl is different. The way the mother treats her is different." Gee, having a baby and being a mother must be really hard and it must really change a person because all I know is that my mother is really different from me.

Terry picks me up Saturday night in her brother's white Mustang. It's been a really busy week. I haven't even seen her since we quit the contest. We had to build the Senior Class Starch Throwing booth.

"Hi, Sam. We're working until ten o'clock on the first shift, OK?" Terry is wearing a triangle denim scarf in her hair, a workshirt and jeans. Her face is flushed from driving with the Mustang's top down and she looks really glamorous.

"Yeah, I thought we weren't going to finish the booth this afternoon. Lucky thing my Dad and Lenny's Dad helped us with the hammering and Valerie's committee got the cardboard painted in time. We kinda ran out of workers because most of the girls . . ." I don't have to finish. Most of the student council girls are getting dressed up for the contest.

"Mrs. Sato and the cafeteria ladies finished cooking the starch and Neal and his friends and some of the football guys are going to carry the big pots of starch over to the booth for us." Terry is in charge of the manpower because she knows everybody.

"Terry's mother is on the phone!" my mother is calling to us from the house. Terry runs in to answer the phone. Funny, her mother always calls my house when Terry is supposed to pick me up. My mother looks out at me from the door. The look on her face says, "Checking up." Terry runs past her and jumps back in the car.

"You're lucky, your mother is really nice," she says.

We go down Kuakini Street and turn onto Liliha. We pass School Street and head down the freeway on-ramp. Terry turns on K-POI and I settle down in my seat. Terry drives faster than my father. We weave in and out of cars as she guns the Mustang down H-1. I know this is not very safe, but I like the feeling in my stomach. It's like going down hills. My hair is flying wild and I feel so clean and good. Like the first day of algebra class before the symbols get mixed up. Like the first day of chemistry before we have to learn molar solutions. I feel like it's going to be the first day forever and I can make the clean feeling last and last. The ride is too short. We turn off by the Board of

Water Supply station and we head down by the Art Academy and turn down Pensacola past Mr. Feiterra's green gardens and into the parking lot of the school.

"I wish you were still in the contest tonight," I tell Terry as we walk out toward the Carnival grounds. "I mean you are so perfect for the Carnival Queen. You were the only Japanese girl that was perfect enough to win."

"I thought you were my friend," Terry starts mumbling. "You sound like my mother. You only like me because of what you think I should be." She starts walking faster and is leaving me behind.

"Wait! What? How come you getting so mad?" I'm running to keep up with her.

"Perfect, perfect. What if I'm NOT perfect. What if I'm not what people think I am? What if I can't be what people think I am?" She's not making any sense to me and she's crying. "Why can't you just like me? I thought you were different. I thought you just liked me. I thought you were my friend because you just liked ME." I'm following her and I feel like it's exam time in chemistry. I'm flunking again and I don't understand.

We get to the Senior booth and Terry disappears behind the cardboard. Valerie Rosecrest is there and hands me a lot of paper cupcake cups and a cafeteria juice ladle.

"Quick, we need at least a hundred of these filled, we're going to be open in ten minutes."

"Try to wait, I gotta find Terry." I look behind the cardboard back of the booth. Terry is not there. I run all around the booth. Terry is nowhere in sight. The Senior booth is under a tent in the midway with all the games. There are lots of lightbulbs strung like kernels of corn on wires inside the tent. There's lots of game booths and rows and rows of stuffed animal prizes on clotheslines above each booth. I can't find Terry and I want to look around more, but all of a sudden the merry-go-round music starts and all the lights come on. The Senior booth with its hand-painted signs, "Starch Throw—three script" looks alive all of a sudden in the warm Carnival light.

"Come on, Sam!" Valerie is calling me. "We're opening. I need you to help!" I go back to the booth. Pretty soon Terry comes back and I look at her kind of worried, but under the soft popcorn light, you cannot even tell she was crying.

"Terry, Mr. Miller said that you're supposed to watch the script can and take it to the cafeteria when it's full." Val's talking to her, blocking my view. Some teachers are arriving for first shift. They need to put on shower caps and stick their heads through holes in the cardboard so students can buy paper cupcake cups full of starch to throw to try to hit the teachers in the face. Terry goes in the back to help the teachers get ready. Lots of guys from my dropout class are lining up in the front of the booth.

"Eh, Sam, come on, take my money. Ogawa's back there. He gave me the F in math. Gimme the starch!" Business is getting better and better all night. Me, Val, and Terry are running around the booth, taking script, filling cupcake cups, and getting out of the way fast when the guys throw the starch. Pretty soon, the grass in the middle of the booth turns into a mess that looks like thrown-up starch, and we are trying not to slip as we run around trying to keep up with business.

"Ladies and gentlemen, McKinley High School is proud to present the 1966 Carnival Queen and her court." It comes over the loudspeaker. It must be the end of the contest, ten o'clock. All the guys stop buying starch and turn to look toward the tent. Pretty soon, everyone in the tent has cleared the center aisle. They clap as five girls in evening dresses walk our way.

"Oh, great," I think. "I have starch in my hair and I don't want to see them." The girls are all dressed in long gowns and are wearing white gloves. The first girl is Linda. She looks so pretty in a maroon velvet A-line gown. Cannot see her musubi-shaped body and her face is just glowing. The rhinestones in her tiara are sparkling under each of the hundreds of carnival lights. The ribbon on her chest says "Third Princess." It's neat! Just like my cousin Carolyn's wedding. My toes are tingling under their coating of starch. The next is Trudye. She's not wearing braces and she looks so pretty in her lavender gown. Some of the guys are going "Wow" under their breath as she walks by. The first Princesses pass next. The Yanagawa twins. They're wearing matching pink gowns and have pink baby roses in their hair, which is in ringlets. Their tiaras look like lace snowflakes on their heads as they pass by. And last.

Even though I know who this is going to be I really want to see her. Sure enough, everybody in the crowd gets quiet as she passes by. Lani looks like her white dress is made of sugar crystals. As she passes, her crown sparkles tiny rainbows under the hundreds of lightbulbs from the tent and flashbulbs popping like little suns.

The court walks through the crowd and stops at the Senior booth. Mr. Harano, the principal, steps out.

"Your majesty," he's talking to Lani, who is really glowing. "I will become a target in the Senior booth in your honor. Will you and your Princesses please take aim and do your best as royal representatives of our school?"

I look around at Terry. The principal is acting so stupid. I can't believe he really runs the whole school. Terry must be getting so sick. But I look at her and she's standing in front of Lani and smiling. This is weird. She's the one who said the contest was fixed. She's the one who said everyone knew who was supposed to win. She's smiling at Lani like my grandmother used to smile at me when I was five. Like I was a sweet mochi[8] dumpling floating in red bean soup. I cannot stand it. I quit the contest so she wouldn't have to quit alone. And she yells at me and hasn't talked to me all night. All I wanted was for her to be standing there instead of Lani.

The Carnival Queen and four Princesses line up in front of the booth. Val, Terry, and I scramble around giving each

[8] steamed rice pounded into a cake

of them three cupcake cups of starch. They get ready to throw. The guys from the newspaper and yearbook get ready to take their picture. I lean as far back into the wall as I can. I know Trudye didn't have time to get contacts yet and she's not wearing any glasses. I wonder where Val is and if she can flatten out enough against the wall to get out of the way. Suddenly, a hand reaches out and grabs my ankle. I look down, and Terry, who is sitting under the counter of the booth with Val, grabs my hand and pulls me down on the grass with them. The ground here is nice and clean. The Carnival Queen and Princesses and the rows of stuffed animals are behind and above us. The air is filled with pink cupcake cups and starch as they throw. Mr. Harano closes his eyes, the flashbulbs go off, but no one comes close to hitting his face. Up above us everyone is laughing and clapping. Down below, Terry, Val, and I are nice and clean.

"Lani looks so pretty, Sam." Terry is looking at me and smiling.

"Yeah, even though the contest was juice she looks really good. Like a storybook," I say, hoping it's not sounding too fake.

"Thanks for quitting with me." Terry's smile is like the water that comes out from between the rocks at Kunawai stream. I feel so clean in that smile.

"It would have been lonely if I had to quit by myself," Terry says, looking down at our starch-covered shoes. She looks up at me and smiles again. And even if I'm covered with starch, I suddenly know that to her, I am beautiful. Her smile tells me that we're friends because I went to dropout class. It is a smile that can wash away all the F's that Mr. Low my chemistry teacher will ever give. I have been waiting all my life for my mother to give me that smile. I know it is a smile that Terry's mother has never smiled at her. I don't know where she learned it.

It's quiet now, the Carnival Queen and her Princesses have walked away. Terry stands up first as she and Val and I start to crawl out from our safe place under the counter of the booth. She gives me her hand to pull me up and I can see her out in the bright Carnival light. Maybe every girl looks like a queen at one time in her life.

A Rice Sandwich

Sandra Cisneros

The special kids, the ones who wear keys around their necks, get to eat in the canteen. The canteen! Even the name sounds important. And these kids at lunch time go there because their mothers aren't home or home is too far away to get to.

My home isn't far but it's not close either, and somehow I got it in my head one day to ask my mother to make me a sandwich and write a note to the principal so I could eat in the canteen too.

Oh no, she says pointing the butter knife at me as if I'm starting trouble, no sir. Next thing you know everybody will be wanting a bag lunch—I'll be up all night cutting bread into little triangles, this one with mayonnaise, this one with mustard, no pickles on mine, but mustard on one side please. You kids just like to invent more work for me.

But Nenny says she doesn't want to eat at school—ever—because she likes to go home with her best friend Gloria who lives across the schoolyard. Gloria's mama has a big color T.V. and all they do is watch cartoons. Kiki and Carlos, on the other hand, are patrol boys. They don't want to eat at school either. They like to stand out in the cold especially if it's raining. They think suffering is good for you ever since they saw that movie *300 Spartans*.

I'm no Spartan and hold up an anemic wrist to prove it. I can't even blow up a balloon without getting dizzy. And besides, I know how to make my own lunch. If I ate at school there'd be less dishes to wash. You would see me less and less and like me better. Everyday at noon my chair would be empty. Where is my favorite daughter you would cry, and when I came home finally at 3 p.m. you would appreciate me.

Okay, okay, my mother says after three days of this. And the following morning I get to go to school with my mother's letter and a rice sandwich because we don't have lunch meat.

Mondays or Fridays, it doesn't matter, mornings always go by slow and this day especially. But lunch time came finally and I got to get in line with the stay-at-school kids. Everything is fine until the nun who knows all the canteen kids by heart looks at me and says: You, who sent you here? And since I am shy, I don't say anything, just hold out my hand with the letter. This is no good, she says, till Sister Superior gives the okay. Go upstairs and see her. And so I went.

I had to wait for two kids in front of me to get hollered at, one because he did something in class, the other because he didn't. My turn came and I stood in front of the big desk with holy pictures under the glass while the Sister Superior read my letter. It went like this:

Dear Sister Superior,

Please let Esperanza eat in the lunch room because she lives too far away and she gets tired. As you can see she is very skinny. I hope to God she does not faint.

Thanking you,
Mrs. E. Cordero

You don't live far, she says. You live across the boulevard. That's only four blocks. Not even. Three maybe. Three long blocks away from here. I bet I can see your house from my window. Which one? Come here. Which one is your house?

And then she made me stand up on a box of books and point. That one? she said pointing to a row of ugly three-flats, the ones even the raggedy men are ashamed to go into. Yes, I nodded even though I knew that wasn't my house and started to cry. I always cry when nuns yell at me, even if they're not yelling.

Then she was sorry and said I could stay—just for today, not tomorrow or the day after—you go home. And I said yes and could I please have a Kleenex—I had to blow my nose.

In the canteen, which was nothing special, lots of boys and girls watched while I cried and ate my sandwich, the bread already greasy and the rice cold.

So's Your Mama

Julie Blackwomon

We were all sitting down the street on Miss Lottie's newly washed steps when Jaimie came by. I think Nikki saw Jaimie first because she yelled, "Hey, Jaimie, bring your ass on down here!" when Jaimie was still almost half a block away. Nikki and Jaimie both play basketball for Southern and have gym and home ec together but it isn't that they're really that tight or anything. It's just that Nikki likes a lot of attention—that's the way Nikki is.

"If you lived on this block you wouldn't be doing all that cussing all up and down the street," Angela said. Angela was sitting on the top step beside Karen.

"All what cussing?" Nikki said in mock innocence. "All I said was ass."

"See, you think it's funny," Angela whined, "but somebody'll be telling my mother we were all down here cussin' and she'll be getting on my case . . ."

"Yeah, beanhead," Sheila chimed in. "Cut out the goddamned cussin'."

"Aw shut up, pepperhead," Nikki said cheerfully.

"You shut up, fart face," Sheila snapped.

"I'd rather be a fart face than a pepperhead," Nikki said.

"Least my family didn't find me on the dump," Sheila said.

I stopped listening to them squabble and turned to watch Jaimie as she approached the steps where we all sat: Nikki, Sheila, Karen, Angela and me. My name's Kathleen but they call me Kippy. School had let out early and we were just hanging out on Miss Lottie's steps shooting the breeze. Earlier we'd been playing hot cold butter beans but Karen's little brother Boo Boo kept standing across the street telling where everyone was hiding. We'd chase him but he'd run and duck behind the parked cars and come right back to pester us again. We would have been jumping doubledutch, but the rope was in Angela's house and Angela's mother was home. If Angela went in now she'd have to stay and finish her homework instead of waiting until seven o'clock when we'd planned on doing it together.

Jaimie was holding her left arm slightly above her eyebrows, shielding her eyes from the three o'clock sun. She must have just left school because she still wore her gymsuit with "Jaimie" stitched in thick yellow thread across the front. Her books were tucked under her arm.

Jaimie doesn't come over to hang out with us too often because she's got a part-time job working behind the counter at the Gino's at Broad and Snyder. And then there's basketball practice. Jaimie plays guard for Southern. She's good too, wiry and fast—a blur of blue uniform and flashing brown arms. I'm always glad when Jaimie comes over to hang out with us though, because I like Jaimie a lot. Nikki says Jaimie's a lesbian, only it's bulldagger when Nikki says it but I don't like to use that word because my mother's a lesbian—which means mostly that my mother has a bunch of women friends and works for the women's bookstore and goes to lots of meetings and demonstrations and stuff, and the only men who get invited to our house for dinner anymore are Grandpop Jones and Uncle Ralph. Only Uncle Ralph isn't really my uncle but the man Mom lived with before she decided she liked women better than men.

"Least my family ain't so poor we gotta eat roach sandwiches," Nikki was saying now. Nikki had an unsharpened yellow pencil behind her left ear. She was sitting on the third from the bottom step and was turned sideways with her back to me, looking up at Sheila who was leaning against the wall beside the steps.

"Least we don't drink snot for Kool Aid," Sheila said, then looked over at me. I smiled and winked at her. Sheila's my best friend. She and Nikki live over in the projects about five blocks from here, but Sheila comes over and we walk to school together every morning. Sheila used to live in Harlem with an aunt. That's because her Mom used to be on junk but she went into the hospital and got herself straightened out, and now she's o.k. I taught Sheila how to bust and she taught me how to fight—how to duck and slide punches. I don't fight much because I'm really too old for that kid stuff. Besides, I don't like to fight and I don't have to anymore because I'm strong and because I showed them as soon as I moved around here that I've got heart so they don't be messin' with me.

"Least I don't have to steal stuff out the garbage can to wear for Easter," Sheila was saying now. Sheila wasn't supposed to have gotten another bust in before Nikki, but I was glad she did. Sheila isn't too good at busting because she keeps taking stuff personal and starts denying. When you're busy denying that keeps the conversation on you. To win you gotta forget about defense and just attack. So if someone says your father's a wino, you just say "least my father don't eat scabs" or something like that. It's not fair to say anything that's really true or to talk about somebody's Mom 'cause that means you really want to fight. Like Karen's Mom's on welfare and Nikki's Pop's in jail but nobody ever brings that up. Nobody talks about my mother being lesbian either.

"You kids make sure you take all your shit off my steps!" Miss Lottie stuck her head out the second floor window and glared down at us. She had a grey scarf tied around her head with a bunch of thick plaits sticking out the top.

"Yes, ma'am," Angela said and balled up her potato chip bag and stuck it in the pocket of the blue jacket she had tied by the sleeves around her waist. Miss Lottie kept glaring at us from the second floor window until Jaimie took Karen's empty Coke bottle and handed it to Karen. Then Miss Lottie pulled her head back in the window and closed it.

Before we moved to Pierce St. my Mom and I lived in a women's collective in West Philly. A collective is a house where five or six women shop for food, cook, do laundry and pay bills together just like a family even though some are black and some are white and some have college degrees and make a lot of money and some don't make much money at all. The first year we lived in the collective four of our housemates took me camping at a women's music festival in Michigan while Mom and Terri went to a black women's conference in N.Y. I liked living in the collective. It was like one big happy family. Only most of the family was white. Shortly before we moved here I got into this rift with this kid and ended up calling his Mom a black dog. And it had nothing to do with bad feelings about being black either. It's just that when someone busts on you and you aren't friends with them or anything, the best thing to do is to bust back on their Mom—either that or punch them in the mouth, because if you don't, the kid'll think you're chicken and they'll mess with you until you prove you aren't. So when this kid called me a black dog I just said, "Your Mom's a black dog!" Just like that. I mean, it was automatic. But I knew I shouldn't have said it. The moment the words passed my lips I got this strange uncomfortable feeling; then when I looked across the street and saw Mom and Terri standing in the doorway I could have just squeezed through a crack in the pavement. I expected Mom to start bombarding me with books about Sojourner Truth and trips to the African History Museum again but she didn't and I thought the thing was over until about a month later she started talking about me moving in with Grandma and I said I didn't want to unless she went too, then Mom said although she and Grandma loved each other, they could never live in the same house again but that I needed to live in a black community and she needed to live in a lesbian feminist community. We compromised by moving here which is three blocks from Grandma. Mom still spends a lot of time over at the collective house, especially when they're doing layout for the newspaper, and sometimes they have meetings at our house. I don't get to go to many women's conferences and stuff with Mom anymore but I still like it here. It's fun spending time with Grandma and Karen lives right across the alleyway from me. Karen's the first person I met when I moved over here. Sometimes she spends the night over my house. I can never spend the night over hers because there's no room. She got six sisters and brothers.

Anyway, after Sheila and Nikki finished busting on

each other Nikki went back to the story she was telling before Jaimie came up. Nikki was standing on the sidewalk now with her foot on the bottom step and she was telling us about the lady who rents a room in her mother's house. Nikki's always telling the woman's business. This time she was saying the woman boarder and some man were in the room with the door locked doing it.

"How do you know the door was locked?" I asked suspiciously. You gotta check on Nikki's stories sometimes, keep her honest. "Did you try the door?"

"Whenever the door's closed it's locked," Nikki said as if she were talking to a four year old.

"So how'd you know they were doing it?" I persisted.

"Well, what else could they have been doing in there with the door locked?" Nikki said.

Then Karen interrupted to say that yesterday Boo Boo was outside on the steps blowing up a rubber.

"What's a rubber?" Angela asked, and everyone started laughing.

Sometimes I feel sorry for Angela. She's kinda quiet and has really short hair that she hardly ever combs so that sometimes it beads up into little knots and it usually takes a long time for her to figure out when someone's putting her on. They were calling her Pepper for almost a year before she put it together that Pepper was short for pepperhead. Mom says that sometimes when black people don't comb their hair it's because they're getting in touch with another part of their ancestral heritage and that's called dreading or wearing dreadlocks but when I told the kids on Pierce St. this they just laughed and said that might be true for some people but that Angela just wasn't into combing her hair.

Anyway, Karen was saying that everybody was busy laughing at Boo Boo who was outside on the front steps blowing up a rubber until her older brother came home, hit Boo Boo up side his head and snatched the rubber. Then when Karen started teasing him about it her older brother lied and said the rubber wasn't even his.

Man, it was really funny the way Karen was telling it—she was running back and forth, first being Boo Boo in his high-pitched whiny voice and then her older brother in a deep growly voice. I'm sure she was making some of it up but that's probably why it was so funny. Karen can really make you crack up.

Then we got to talking about who'd seen a rubber and who hadn't. Everyone said they'd seen one, even me, although I hadn't really. But it was o.k. though, because I had seen a penis, or two if you want to count the Christmas when Uncle Ralph still lived with us and the buttons of his old red pajamas came loose. The other penis I saw just last summer. It belonged to my cousin Kenny who's fifteen and just starting to shave. I was helping him pick corn in my Grandfather's cornfield in Virginia when Kenny just pulled it out and peed as if I wasn't even there. I turned my head at first then snuck another peek. Kenny looked over his shoulder and said, "What you lookin' at squirt." Then he laughed and shoved it in his pants and we went back to picking corn.

The sun had gone down and the steps were getting chilly under my butt and I wanted to go home and get my jacket but I didn't want to leave because it was getting late and everybody would be going in for dinner soon anyway. Besides, Jaimie might be gone when I got back. So I just got up off the chilly steps and jumped around on thc sidewalk a little. I was trying to work up enough nerve to ask Jaimie if I could put on her jacket which was still lying on the steps on top of her books, but before I'd gotten it together to ask, Karen had picked it up and draped it across her knees without even asking Jaimie if it was o.k. first.

Then somebody started talking about doing it and nobody was saying much because Karen was doing most of the talking and Karen's a smart ass. Karen'll tell you a really good story, let you tell one, then turn around and say hers wasn't true at all and that she'd only just now made it up. Then she'd crack up. She's a real comedian.

I think Jaimie was getting restless. She'd put on her jacket which she'd taken back from Karen and was standing around with her hands making lumps in her jeans like she was ready to go. I was getting pissed with myself because I hadn't said anything at all to her except "hello" and then Nikki startled me by calling my name.

"Hey, Kippy," Nikki yelled, "some dude's going into your house."

I followed the direction of her gaze and sure enough,

someone was standing on my steps and leaning on the side railing with their back to us. From the distance I couldn't tell who it was at first but then I recognized Terri's pea jacket and white tam.

"So what?" Angela said. "You a newspaper reporter or something?"

"Ain't nobody even talking to you, Angela," Nikki said.

"That ain't no dude anyway," Karen said with a little giggle. "That's a woman."

"That's a dude," Nikki said.

"That's a woman, stupid," Angela said.

Nikki turned to me. "Ain't that a dude on your steps, Kippy?"

"Terri ain't no dude!" I said.

"Well, if it ain't no dude, it's got to be a bulldagger," Nikki said.

"And what's a bulldagger?" I asked sarcastically.

"You don't know what a bulldagger is?" Nikki giggled, and elbowed Karen in the ribs.

"No, what's a bulldagger?" I said, my hands on my hips, my nose now only inches away from Nikki's.

"Well," Nikki said equally sarcastic, "a bulldagger's a freak."

"And what's a freak?"

"A freak's a woman who wants to be a man."

"Well, Terri don't want to be no man. She doesn't even like men."

"Then why she dress like a man?"

"She don't dress like no man; she's just got on pants. Everybody wears pants."

"Right," Nikki said. "Everybody wears pants—including bulldaggers."

Somebody snickered and Karen said, "Nikki, why don't you shut up?"

"You shut up," Nikki said without turning to look at Karen. The other girls were now in a circle around us and Boo Boo and some of the younger kids who'd been playing down the street had now come up to stand around and watch.

"Your mother wears pants," I said.

"Yeah, my mother wears pants, but my mother's got a boyfriend too."

Nikki looked over at Karen, then quickly back at me. Karen looked down at her feet. Suddenly it dawned on me: we weren't talking about Terri; we were talking about my mother.

"Look," I said slowly—I felt sad and kinda tired. "Just because you don't have a boyfriend and wear pants doesn't mean you want to be a man . . ."

The words trailed off and stopped. I wanted to add "Yeah, my mother's a lesbian but she isn't a bulldagger; she doesn't want to be a man." I wanted to say "Yeah, Terri's a lesbian and most of my mother's friends are lesbians but there's nothing wrong with that—it doesn't mean anybody wants to be a man." But it just didn't seem right to say it right then and there in front of Nikki with all the other kids gaping on and probably agreeing with Nikki that lesbians and bulldaggers are the same thing when it isn't that way at all. But I didn't know how to make them understand that it was really o.k. and I felt kinda dumb and stupid because I didn't know how to make them see. And I felt disloyal to my mother, kinda like I'd feel if I were high yaller and in an all-white class and someone said something nasty about blacks and I didn't say anything back. And then I was really mad at Nikki all over again because I felt like she'd busted on my Mom on the sly and because I was scared I was gonna cry right there in front of everybody and it was all Nikki's fault. And I wanted to punch her in the mouth but she was skinny and I knew I could beat her. I wanted to call her a barrel of blitzing bitches but then I didn't want to because Mom says it isn't nice to call girls and women bitches, but mostly I wanted to anyway because I was really mad and sometimes when you're really mad at someone, calling them a few bitches or mother-fuckers is as good as a swift rap in the mouth—though I don't usually cuss unless I'm really mad or just showing off. And now I was just standing around with my teeth clenched trying to decide what to do, and my left leg was trembling so bad I was afraid someone would see it and think I was trembling because I was scared and not just because I always tremble when I get real mad. But before I decided what to do I heard Jaimie's voice from behind me.

"Nikki, why don't you just shut your face and go home."

"This is a free country!" Nikki said.

"Look, Nikki," I said, totally ignoring Jaimie's interference, "you and me can go settle this in the schoolyard!" I took off my sweater and threw it to the sidewalk.

Nikki hesitated, then took half a step backward. "You better get out of my face, girl," she said.

"It ain't your face I'm interested in," I said, both hands on my hips and patting my foot. "I'm gonna kick your ass."

"It ain't about no fighting, Kippy."

"Oh it's about fighting alright. Sounds like you been talking about fighting real loud." I inched up closer until I was right up in her face. Her nose was blurred from being so close and I could feel her warm breath on my cheek.

"Sounds like you'll be thinking I'm some kind of chickenshit if I don't knock you on your skinny ass!"

"I got no reason to fight you, Kippy," Nikki said and stuck her nose up in the air like she was Cleopatra and I was a fly buzzing around her head. This made me madder.

"Yeah, you want to fight me alright," I said. "You want to fight me real bad!" I gave her a little shove on the shoulders.

"Look, I'm going home," Nikki said and turned and started weaving her way through the circle of kids behind her.

"You come back here, you bitch," I said and grabbed her by the back of the sweater. But she pulled away.

I skipped a few steps behind her and pushed her but she kept walking. I wanted to call her another bitch, wanted to go after her, maybe push her again but I was beginning to feel mean, like I was picking on her or something. So I just stood there and watched her walking off with her nose in the air like everyone else had disappeared and she was the only one on the street.

Sheila picked up my sweater from the sidewalk and handed it to me and I brushed if off and draped it across my arm. I was still cold but for some reason I didn't want to put the sweater on. Then Angela mumbled something about getting her butt on home and then she and the rest of the gang kinda wandered off one or two at a time until only Sheila, Jaimie and I were left standing in a half-circle with our hands in our pockets. A kid whizzed by on a bright yellow ten speed bike and I could smell chicken cooking in somebody's house.

"You should have punched her in the mouth," Sheila said.

"Yeah, I should have," I said softly and without much conviction.

"I don't know that it would have done any good," Jaimie said.

"No, I guess not," I said.

"But it might have made you feel better," Jaimie said with a smile.

"Yeah, I guess so," I said.

I was agreeing with everything everybody said and for

some reason that struck me as really funny, so I just burst out laughing. Sheila and Jaimie looked at each other and started laughing, too, mostly at me, I think. And then we were all laughing hard, much harder than anything was funny but for some reason I just couldn't stop. It was getting dark and people were walking by and giving us strange looks and that only made us laugh some more.

American Bandstand

Denise Sherer Jacobson

I hated nice weather. My mother would make me sit on the stone stoop of our brown apartment building after the school bus dropped me off, while she gossiped with the neighbors. She said it would do me good to get a little sun—I was so pale and skinny.

"But Ma," I whined, "I want to go up and watch 'American Bandstand.'" "Bandstand" was to the '60s and '70s what "Soul Train" was to the '80s and MTV's "The Grind" is to the '90s.

"It will still be on by the time we go up. Look, your sister will be home from school in a few minutes and I'll send her to the candy store to get you a chocolate malted." My mother was not above bribery.

So I sat listening to the droning voices being carried into the air as the women talked about the fruit in season at the grocer or the sale on bathing suits at Alexander's. I cooed at the babies awake in their strollers and felt pleased with myself that I could make them smile and laugh—they weren't old enough to know I was different. And I watched as the kids walked past in droves as they were let out of neighborhood schools, the younger ones who would stare at me as their mothers ushered them on and the older ones who'd try not to notice me at all. I tried to ignore it all.

I would reach over to my navy blue and red plastic bookbag sitting next to me on the steps and pull out a book, usually a Nancy Drew or, if my book report was due soon, one of the classics—a Mark Twain or Louisa May Alcott. Reading had its purposes—keeping me occupied and, by burying my nose in a book, I thought I could forget that Leslie Strom was on her way and I wouldn't have to see her snub me. Only it never worked. I could always hear her coming—step-clump, step-clump, on the concrete sidewalk—even above the kids' screechy voices and the heavy car traffic of the Grand Concourse. Step-clump.

"There goes Gimpy again," I grumbled one day to Shelley, not loud enough for Mommy to hear.

"You know her?" My sister was surprised.

"We ride together in the same van to the Carolians' on Saturdays. Yech." I felt much the same about the Carolian Club as I did about the sun, but my mother insisted it was good for me to go. Yet if I had to choose between the two,

I'd rather fry in the sun. "She never speaks to me in the van, either."

My sister offered compassion: "Hey, maybe one day, I'll run upstairs and throw a bucket of water out the window when she passes by."

I chuckled. Shelley could think such wicked thoughts. I wished one day she'd really have the guts to do it. I could just imagine Leslie caught in the cascade—her carefully combed flip flopping, while water dripped from her stringy bangs and down her upturned nose. It would serve her right—that polio gimp.

I didn't like her snubbing me, but I understood it. I was just letting my jealousy get the best of me. Oh, I wasn't jealous of her because she only walked with one leg brace while I walked with crutches and double-leg braces connected by a pelvic band—although my braces weighed about three times as much as hers. They only really bothered me when the weather was hot and the leather bands holding my legs in place stuck to my skin, or when, as a growing eleven year old, I would outgrow them every four to six months—the pelvic band would press into my hips and irritate the skin covering my pelvic bone until the readjustment could be made. Yet, besides holding up my knee socks, my braces gave me a steadiness, a feeling of security and brief moments of pleasure, feeling such heavenly relief and freedom when I took them off at night. No, it wasn't her brace or ability to walk better . . .

It wasn't that she was able to go to a neighborhood

school, either. I got more attention in the special unit I was bussed to everyday than I would have in a regular classroom. All my teachers (of which I only had three since kindergarten) were very impressed with me, and why not? I was smarter and cuter than the other handicapped kids; in the sixth grade, I was reading at a high school level, and I was still blond and had a small nose. My mother always made sure I sparkled when I went to school in the morning (not that I'd come home the same way)—a little doll, they called me, since I was small and fragile-looking; they even remarked that when I sat still at my desk, you couldn't tell there was anything wrong with me. So what if the other kids at school didn't like me—the ones my age teased me because I was teacher's pet, and the kids in my class—teenagers—didn't want a little squirt hanging around. No matter, adults were more important than those snotty kids; they appreciated me. If I went to a neighborhood school like Leslie, I'd just get lost in the crowd.

No, what really bothered me about Leslie was that she was acceptable—her, and the clique she hung out with on Saturdays. True, the girls were a little older—twelve or thirteen—but the fact of the matter was, older or younger, they could all do whatever they wanted to. They'd get permission to leave the clubhouse and hang out at the corner hamburger joint. They'd get the leads in every drama group production. And none of the staff ever "found" them when they hid under a stairwell smoking cigarets. They were doing just what was expected of them, because they only had polio—a mere inconvenience that surely didn't stop any of them from being average kids. After all, they didn't have to just sit still at their desks to look like there was nothing wrong with them—just sitting down ANYWHERE would do.

The polios—they were always at the top of the ladder, while I was on the bottom rung, because I had cerebral palsy (c.p.). The I.Q. tests didn't matter; any movements in your body that you couldn't control, speech that was slurred or slow, placed you on the bottom. No matter how I tried to climb up that ladder I still had the wrong disability. I hobbled too slowly to go with them to the candy store—even if they wanted me to, which, of course, they didn't. I'd lip a cigaret if I took a drag, since my mouth always seemed to have an excess of saliva which escaped down my chin if I didn't remember to swallow. And then there was drama . . .

Drama was the one activity I wanted so desperately to be in. I knew I'd be good; I was such a natural—I could have a smile on my face even when I was miserable, make people laugh with my "wonderful sense of humor," poking fun at myself before others got the chance: "I walk so slow even the Tortoise could beat me in a race." I was a great actress—alone in my room—playing out romantic scenarios: princesses, captured by tyrants, rescued by handsome princes. I told myself my speech impairment didn't matter; when people really listened, it wasn't hard to understand me (my speech therapist even said so): if I were up there on stage, my audience would have nothing else to do but listen.

Still, I wouldn't dare try out for a part. I could just hear what would be said about me: "She's making a fool out of herself, just like the rest of them." Then the head of the Carolians would get wind of it and note in my file: "The child is immature and has an unrealistic view of her limitations. She does not accept her handicap." Inevitably, the comment would appear on my school, medical and camp records and I would be lumped together with all the other c.p.'s. I couldn't let that happen. So, I proved that I was not only smart, but knew my place, too—I joined the club newspaper.

My mother's voice took me out of my silent lament: "Shelley, I want you to go get Neisie a malted."

"Aw, Ma, send one of the other kids, send Nancy, she's just hanging around," protested my chubby sister, slapping her books down on the stone stoop. "I told Harriet I'd meet her at her house."

It was always Harriet, or Alice, or Barbara. It was only me as a last resort—on weekend mornings when no one else was around. I knew she'd rather play with kids her own age but I was only two years and nine months younger and, I thought, a lot nicer than any of her friends—they were always so snotty. They'd only let me play with them on rainy days when their mothers gathered in our apartment to play mah-jongg.

The kids would go off into my parents' bedroom after

the women chased them away for pestering them at the game. My mother, like the others, would be so glad to not have them breathing down her neck that she'd give the kids permission to do anything—play with make-up? "okay"; wear old dresses and high heels? "alright"; jewelry? "only costume"; and she'd call after them, "Let Neisie play."

On all fours—my way of getting around without my braces (a wheelchair was unheard of; my mother was afraid I'd start depending on it too much)—I'd half hop, half creep into the bedroom. They would be all dressed up in pinks and blues, fake pearls and rhinestones.

"Here," one of them would say, throwing the ugliest dark, ragged housedress over me. "You can be the wicked witch or the evil stepmother."

"Can't I be the fairy godmother?" I asked, already blinking back stinging tears.

"Nancy's the fairy godmother."

"You always let her be that," I pouted. They were always nicer to Nancy. Not that they really wanted to be—they were just scared of her mother: Pearlie could intimidate them with just one look. "Why am I always the evil stepmother?"

"Because we said so . . . And if you don't like it, you won't play," came the final ultimatum.

It was no use looking to my sister for help; she stayed silent. I knew if I cried to my mother, she'd yell at Shelley, who would take it out on me. Besides, my mother was no

Pearlie when it came to discipline; she'd just end up trying to make me understand, "Neisie, kids are cruel."

So, I played the evil stepmother, ordering them to mop the floors and wash the dishes. They, of course, ran away, clunking off in oversized high heels. I followed after them, trying not to get my knees black-and-blue thudding them down too hard on the bedroom's linoleum floor, or get splinters in my hands as I crept over the wooden hump of the doorway, or get rug burns from creeping on the living room carpet.

I couldn't keep up with them; my legs kept getting caught in the stupid old housedress. Soon, a familiar muscle in the back of my neck would go into one quick spasm, in protest of all my tensely driving motion. The cramp jerked my head back, lasting no more than a second or two, but the pain was so deep that it sent hot shivers up to my head and down my spine. No one was paying attention to notice, so I would just sit there until the funny tingling went away. All that remained was my headache, which had really started before the chase. I'd have to ask my mother for aspirin and then go lie down. Dress-up time was over anyway; the kids were playing 45's.

I had just slurped down the last of the malted that Nancy had volunteered to get for me because Shelley had gone off to Harriet's. Looking up at my mother's heavyset frame leaning against the stoop, I called until she heard me. "Ma? Ma?"

"What, Neisie?" Her head turned downward, but I

couldn't see her face—the sun was in my eyes. "You're drooling, honey. You have to remember to swallow. You know what I always tell you?"

"Yes, Ma." I recited with boredom: "When someone says I'm cute and takes my chin in their hand and feels that it's all wet, they'll go 'blech!'" I made a horrible face.

"Right. And they won't want to do it anymore." She turned away for a moment to hear what a neighbor was saying.

"Good," I mumbled to myself, "let 'em keep their hands to themselves." Still, I wiped my chin on the sleeve of my furry, red jacket before my mother saw me. Otherwise, she'd scold me, saying that the saliva would ruin the fur. I always did it, anyhow, when no one was looking—too lazy to pull out the hankie from my pocket. I finished seconds before she looked back at me. She waited while I swallowed.

"Ma, can we go up now?"

She clucked her tongue in mild exasperation. "Well, I guess I ought to start making supper soon, so we can eat before Daddy gets home. Just let me have one more cigaret."

"But, Ma, I'll miss Record Review." They sometimes had it in the first half hour of "Bandstand" just like they do the top ten music videos on "The Grind."

"Neisie, be patient," my mother mildly admonished. "We're going soon." I threw my book back into my book-bag, snapped it shut and waited. It took her forever to finish.

Putting the butt out on the stone stoop and throwing it out into the gutter (for the street cleaners to sweep up in the morning), she gathered my aluminum crutches, my bookbag, her purse. She held it all with her right arm and hand, leaving her other limb free. I offered my right wrist, which her free hand grasped. She pulled me to my feet; it always took me a few seconds to stop wobbling. Then, using her body to steady her arm as she held me, we started the climb—22 stone steps on the outside, 20 marble steps to go once inside the hallway. By the time we were on the fourteenth or fifteenth marble step, the back of my legs would ache from the strain of carrying not only my own weight and the weight of my braces, but with the anticipation that in a few more steps, the grueling climb would be over.

Afraid that if I sat down on the kitchen chair, I'd be too wiped out to get up, I remained standing against the threshold of the kitchen and reached for my crutches propped against a nearby wall. Still catching my breath, I positioned the worn rubber armrests under my armpits and placed my hands tightly around the wooden handles. I hobbled my way through the long foyer to the living room (always filled with the musty film of cigaret smoke) and into the rectangular, blue-walled bedroom that I shared with my sister.

Immediately, I went to the television corner to switch on channel 7—"American Bandstand"—to be with Peggy and Justine and Bob and Tony and all my other friends. It didn't matter that I wasn't fourteen; I was mature for my age. I didn't even play with dolls—I couldn't dress them with all their buttons, buckles and bows.

While the TV warmed up, I leaned my crutches alongside the window and plopped down on the bed. A Clearasil commerical was on followed by station identification giving me just enough time to rest and wipe the sweat from my forehead. Then I stood up and, holding on to whatever was steady in between, inched my way over to the closet. Grasping the doorknob, I was ready for the next cha-cha to Frankie Avalon's "Venus," or Lindy hop to Connie Francis' "Lipstick on Your Collar." I thought I wasn't that bad, either—keeping time with the one-two but leaving the cha-cha-cha (or else I'd lose the beat) and, of course, I didn't swirl around too much during the Lindy. I sat out the slow dances, since there was no shoulder to lean on; instead, I'd sing along with the Platters' "Smoke Gets in Your Eyes"—I could keep up with most of the words—and was proud that I was able to carry a tune.

What a relief!! No one stared. No one teased. No one disapproved—at least for the rest of the hour.

from THE SUNITA EXPERIMENT

MITALI PERKINS

When Sunita got home that afternoon, she found a note on the kitchen table. "Bontu," it said, "gone to meet Dad in the city. Leftover curry in fridge for dinner. Love, Mom, Didu, and Dadu."

It was strangely quiet in the house. The mail had arrived, and she flipped through it idly. A huge red envelope in the shape of a heart caught her eye. Big block letters across the front announced, "Mrs. Ria Majumdar—You and Your Date Can Win a Free Weekend in New York City!" The return address said, "The *Endless Hope* Plot Solution Contest, Star Television Studios, New York, New York." Sunita grinned as she put the envelope on her grandmother's pillow.

She wandered out into the back yard. The sky had cleared up after lunch, but new storm clouds were gathering over the hills. The wind rattled the trees, shaking down a layer of golden leaves over Dadu's flower beds. Sunita shivered and turned back inside as drops of rain began to fall again. She watched until it became a steady downpour and then dialed Liz's number.

"Mrs. Grayson? I guess the track meet must have been canceled by now. Is Liz home yet?"

"Sorry, Sunni. Liz just called. Get this. Both teams were all geared up to compete, so they decided to find a way to battle it out indoors. At this very moment, they are locked in mortal combat—at the bowling alley! I'm leaving right now to go shopping, and I'm supposed to pick her up in a couple of hours."

After turning down Mrs. Grayson's offer to drop her off at the bowling alley, Sunita sat down and finished her homework. Sunita Sen, social flop. The only teenager in America with nothing better to do on a Friday afternoon than her homework. She slammed her notebook shut, realizing that she hadn't watched *Casablanca* in a long time.

Sam, the black piano player, was pouring his heart into their favorite song. Sunita sat back, ready to lose herself in one of her favorite scenes.

But she just couldn't seem to get into it. All kinds of questions she'd never asked before kept popping into her head. Didn't Sam have a life of his own? Why did he have to call her Miss Ilsa when she just called him Sam? Where was Casablanca anyway? Wasn't it in Africa? Why were there no black Africans in the entire movie? And why was she starting to sound like Mr. Riley?

Mr. Riley had spent the past week asking them to identify cultural and racial stereotypes in popular movies. The class had enjoyed watching current videos and discussing them. They were going to look at some classic children's books next week.

Sunita turned off the movie and headed upstairs with a determined look in her eye.

When Geetie came home, Sunita was curled up on the couch under an afghan, frowning over a battered old copy of *The Secret Garden*.

Sunita followed her sister into the kitchen. "This used to be my favorite book in the whole world," she announced.

"Isn't it still?" Geetie asked, peering into the fridge past the chicken curry. "When is Mom going to get it through her head that I'm a vegetarian?" she grumbled.

"Listen to this." Sunita began to read.

"It's different in India," said Mistress Mary disdainfully. She could scarcely stand this.

But Martha was not at all crushed.

"Eh! I can see it's different," she answered almost sympathetically. "I dare say it's because there's such a lot o' blacks there instead o' respectable white people. When I

heard you was comin' from India I thought you was a black too."

Mary sat up in bed furious.

"What!" she said. "What! You thought I was a native. You—you daughter of a pig!"

She slapped the book shut. "Can you believe that?" she demanded.

Geetie's voice came out of the depths of the fridge where she was foraging for tofu. "Don't get disillusioned, kid. Frances Burnett was a product of her time. India was under British rule for years, you know. You can still appreciate the story."

"I guess so. It just makes me mad that I never noticed all this stuff before!"

Something in Sunita's voice made Geetie pull her head out of the fridge. Sunita braced herself for a lecture. Instead, her sister put one hand lightly against Sunita's cheek.

"Welcome to the real world, Bontu," she said softly.

from PETER

KATE WALKER

Vince suggested the subdivision as a good place for taking the photographs of David's car.

"It'll make a good background," he said. "Uncluttered."

We were in our driveway, loading my camera gear into the trunk of the E. H.

"David may not like it," I said. "The kids'll be all over his new paint job."

"You know most of them, don't you?" David asked me.

"My knowing them won't make any difference. They're creeps. Real pea-brains," I said.

"Three of us against twenty of them?" Vince said. "They haven't got a chance." And he stood around smirking, waiting for me to come up with another excuse for not going. What could I say with David there?

When the car rolled into the subdivision, kids came from everywhere, riding across the vacant blocks.

David back-throttled. “I see what you mean,” he said, watching as the mob converged on us.

It wasn’t too late, we could still go somewhere else.

“In the middle there,” Vince said. “That’d be a good place to set up the camera. Then you’d have those long straights to come down and Peter could get some action shots.” That’s what David had liked most about my photos of the bikes.

We pulled up where Vince said, and from the back seat I watched David go through the slow ritual of switching off the ignition, pulling on the handbrake and unclipping his seatbelt. All with the same graceful movements he’d used at our dinner table the Friday before.

Better keep your hands in your pockets here, mate.

Fortunately, he’d come underdressed that day in a T-shirt, long baggy shorts and hairy legs. Eddy might have recognized him as the bloke I was doing the shopping with, but Eddy wasn’t here. Eddy wasn’t ever going to be here again. I’d looked in the newspaper on Saturday and, sure enough, there was his bike for sale, going cheap. Not that I was tempted.

The kids were more interested in the car than anything else. They milled around it, making stupid comments.

"Ace machine!"

"What a fang!"[1] (Which it isn't!)

One dummy even told David he should paint a picture of a dragon devouring a naked chick on the hood.

"Yeah," David answered in a gruff voice. He knew what he was dealing with now, and he kept his arms folded and his hands tucked under his armpits.

Naturally, he towered over all the pygmies. Gaz was the only one who could have matched him for height, and Gaz was there, but he kept to the footpath, watching from the sidelines. When he was a little red-haired kid in primary school, Gaz was exactly the same: if he couldn't be the center of attention, he didn't want to play.

David answered all the boys' questions about the car, while keeping an eagle eye on handlebars and broken foot-pegs passing dangerously close to his new duco. I set up the camera on its tripod in the middle of the road, and when I asked him to take the car back along one of the far streets, he went in a hurry, grateful to get away.

A few kids on BMXs trundled after him as he drove off. I yelled at them to keep out of the picture, and that kept them back. I took several shots with the telephoto lens, panning on the car, keeping it in focus while blurring the background. My hands weren't as steady as I would have liked.

From behind me I heard a few snickers about the bus shelter, nothing blatant. It was possible the labeling hadn't

[1] Australian slang for *fantastic*

stuck as badly as I'd thought. The boys had no *real* reason to think I was gay, it'd all been drummed up out of nothing, and my death-defying ride down the hill-climb might have saved me. After all, it *was* supposed to be the poofter[2] test, and I'd passed it, and half of them hadn't even tried.

Vince being there kept the kids a bit more respectful, of course. He's not physically big but he gives out heavy vibes when he wants to, posing in his sunnies and blowing cigarette smoke out his nose.

I would have had to come down to the subdivision eventually. I wasn't so stupid as to think I could go back to school without putting in an appearance here first, to show that I wasn't scared, and that nothing *they* said was going to faze me. I just would have felt more comfortable doing it my way, in my helmet and boots, with my bike beneath me.

But I was here now, so I concentrated on taking good pictures, and ignored everything else.

It was a top day for photography: bright sunshine, with just a few clouds to cut the glare. Hot as hell, though. All the tar and bare dirt in the subdivision held the heat, and I could feel it rising through the soles of my sneakers.

The kids drifted over to join Gaz on the footpath. It was the usual crowd: Jason, Slacko, Clinton, Joel. Mostly they talked cars. I noticed that Rats was absent. *How lucky can you get?*

[2] derogatory slang term for homosexuals

When I'd taken enough distance shots, I signaled to David to bring the car back, and he pulled up on the far side of the road, as far as possible from the boys. I still had the telephoto lens on the camera and took a picture of him getting out of the car. Then wished I hadn't. It embarrassed him to death. As he came up to me, he smiled. "Just the car, hey?"

Don't smile at me here! And for God's sake, don't wink!

I got really serious about the photographs after that, took shots from ground level, that sort of thing. Made a spectacle of myself generally, and got ripped off about it.

"Get a load of the hotshot photographer!"

"Smile! It's *Candid Camera*!"

"Gunna take our picture too, Pete?"

Good idea! I swung the camera on them and, through the lens, watched them climb on each other's shoulders and pull stupid poses.

The shutter opened and there, riding in from infinity on a decrepit old bicycle, was Rats. Someone must have gone off and told him we were here.

I turned back to the car and kept on taking pictures, waiting to hear him join the group behind me.

"Where's Alice?" his cackling voice said.

"Alice ain't here!"

"He doesn't know what he's missin' out on."

Etc., etc.

It wasn't the sort of conversation Vince or David could have made any sense of, but the kids snickered a lot.

"How many pictures have you taken now?" David asked, when I'd worked my way back to where he and Vince were standing.

"Sixteen," I said.

"That's plenty. I only wanted one or two."

"No. To get one really good shot, you have to take the whole roll," I said, and I kept on going.

I had to look after myself here. If I shot through the instant Rats turned up, I'd never get him off my back. I fiddled with the light meter, adjusted aperture settings, ignored the heat and the sun biting into the back of my neck, and took pictures.

Only twenty frames to go!

"Spiffy little photographer, isn't he, fellers?" Rats said, and there were mumbles of agreement. The kids were being cautious.

Rats never is. "Make a good hairdresser, too!" he added.

I saw David turn his head to glance in Rats's direction.

"Or an interior decorator!"

David's lips moved as he murmured something to Vince. Vince took out his cigarette pack and lit another smoke. This wasn't hurting him; he wasn't in the firing line.

"They go through boyfriends real fast," Rats yelled, "them interior decorators!" There were more laughs. He was picking up supporters.

David stood with his arms folded, squinting a bit.

His hair hung low over his eyes. Possibly he heard this sort of thing all the time from the macho engineering blokes at uni.

I cheated, took a couple of shots of the ground, and wandered back. "That's it," I said.

David nodded. "Might as well go then. Do you need a hand to put your gear away?" The only sign he gave of being uneasy was that he jangled his car keys in his hand.

"You reckon he's got a client waitin'?" Rats said. "Wonder how many he's done so far. We should be gettin' a commission. I bet he's makin' a fortune."

I packed my camera in its case and gave it to David to hold, and Vince asked, "Who's the smart-arse with the suicide complex?"

"Rats, his name is," I said as I folded the tripod.

"Is he the one who started it?" he asked.

"Yeah, sort of."

"Is he a friend of yours?" David said. It was a stupid question, but I guess he needed to say something too. I wasn't sure how much he knew about my problem—being labeled. I didn't know if it was the sort of thing Vince would tell him.

"Rats hasn't got any friends," I said.

"Good," Vince said, "you're in luck then. Go surprise the little jerk. Knock his teeth down his throat."

"No!"

David agreed with me. "His type aren't worth the trouble," he said.

"These Valley View turkeys sure stick together!" Rats said. "D'you reckon they've got a clubhouse and go on picnics? Hey, anyone for a poofter's picnic, leaving now?" Then he started whistling a song we all knew from school, one about homosexual stuff: bums for sale, etc. David probably didn't know it because he didn't go to school here. But from the way the boys carried on, snickering, and even acting things out, the joke was pretty obvious.

"Leave it too much longer, Ace, and you're going to have to take on the lot of them," Vince said, "not just him."

David walked away. He didn't want any part of this. And neither did I.

"You're just like Dad," I said to Vince. "You think every problem can be solved by thumpin' someone."

"You wouldn't need to thump him if you hadn't waited this long."

David opened the trunk of the car and put the camera case inside.

"So where you gunna hide when you go back to school?" Vince said to me. "The girls' toilets?"

"Geez, David must be hard up for friends," I said, "having to knock around with you."

"That kid's a bloody dishrag, Ace. Look at him! You're twice his size. Go mop up the subdivision with him."

The boys must have wondered what we were doing, standing there, whispering at each other.

"He fights dirty," I said.

"Fight dirtier! He's got your number and he's gunna

hound you to death. You won't shut him up any other way."

"If he bothers you, *you* thump him," I said.

He eyed me off through his tinted lenses, then handed me his smokes pack. "OK. Here, hold these."

"No!"

"Get it over with, then, while I'm here to back you up. Don't be a wimp all your life." He didn't take off his sunnies; he never intended fighting Rats for me, he was just trying to shame me into it.

I glanced at David. Did he think I was scared too?

I'm not usually a doer, so when I act, people often get a shock. Rats sure did.

from Finding My Voice

Marie G. Lee

"Moooo!" It is still dark when I reach to shut off the Holstein-shaped alarm clock that my best friend, Jessie, gave me for my sixteenth birthday. To shut it off, you have to pull down on the cow's enormous plastic udder. Mom wanted to throw it out. I told her it was just humor, Jessie-style.

I step into the steamy shower and let the warmth coax me awake. I shampoo, shave my legs, and let the conditioner sit in my hair for exactly five minutes, just as it says on the bottle. After toweling off, I put on deodorant, foot powder, perfume, and then begin applying wine-colored eyeliner under my lashes.

Do boys have to go through all this trouble day in and

day out? How about Tomper Sandel, the football player who appears to be naturally cute with his shaggy blond hair and cleft chin—does he worry about how he smells?

I put on extra eye shadow in a semicircle around my top eyelid. According to *Glamour* magazine, this will give Oriental eyes a look of depth. I've always known that I don't have the neat crease at the top of my lid—like my friends do—that tells you exactly where the eye shadow should stop. So every day I have to paint in that crease, but I don't think I'm fooling anybody.

"Hurry up, Ellen," Mom calls from downstairs. I throw on my new Ocean Pacific T-shirt and jeans and run down.

Mom is standing in the kitchen, quietly spreading peanut butter on whole-wheat bread. She turns to look at me, and her eyebrows dip into a slight frown.

"Is that what you're wearing to school?"

"Yes, Mom," I say. We go through this scene every year.

"What about all those good clothes we bought in Minneapolis?"

"Those dresses are great," I say. "But no one wears a dress on the first day of school."

"Oh," Mom says, as if she's not convinced. She turns to finish packing my lunch. As usual, Father has already left for the hospital so he can get an early start on patients with morning-empty, surgery-ready stomachs.

I grab the Cheerios and milk, and eat while looking

over my schedule one more time. This year, I won't have Jessie in a single class. She took typing and creative foods so that she can have more free time. In the meantime, I'll be sweating out calculus and trying to tack gymnastics onto my already-stuffed schedule. My parents say I have to take all the hard classes so I can get into Harvard like my sister, Michelle.

"Here's your lunch," Mom says, handing me a brown paper bag. I open it and find a small container filled with soft white ovals in sugary liquid.

"What is this?" I grimace, holding the tiny container aloft.

"Litchi nuts," Mom answers. "Remember? You love them."

"Not for lunch," I say, a little too vehemently. The truth is, I don't want people seeing those foreign-looking nuts and asking what they are.

Then I remember that every day Mom packs Father's lunch, then my lunch, while I'm up in the bathroom doing my deodorant-perfume-powder dance.

"Well, thanks, though, Mom," I say. "Could I please have a Hershey's bar from now on?"

Mom smiles. She is so thin and small in her gown and robe. I throw my lunch in my knapsack and kiss her quickly.

"Goodbye, Myong-Ok. It's your last year here," she says. I look up at her, upon hearing my Korean name. To me, it doesn't sound like my name, but to Mom, I think it means something special. Sometimes, I think she has so much to say to me, but it gets lost, partly because of the gap separating Korean and English, and partly because of some other kind of gap that has always existed between me and my parents.

On the way to the bus stop, I slip the container of litchi nuts into a garbage can alongside the road. Wasteful, I know, but I'm always so nervous on the first day of school. All those kids. Especially the popular ones.

Everyone is at the bus stop—the same faces from last year, and the year before, and the year before that, but my throat still constricts. I wish Jessie lived nearby so she could take the bus with me. Two of the hockey players, Brad Whitlock and Mike Anderson, are loudly hooting and swaggering as if they own the place. I slip back and try to become invisible.

When the bus comes, student bodies swarm around the door like eager bees waiting to get into the hive. I let most of the kids go ahead of me, but as I board, someone shoves me from behind.

"Hey chink, move over."

In back of me is Brad Whitlock, a darkly adult look clouding his face. The sound of his words hangs for a moment in the cramped air of the school bus. Numbly, I look around. Everyone seems to be looking somewhere else: out the window, at their books, just away. Brad pushes past me to the back of the bus, where he resumes guffawing with his friends.

I sit gingerly in the nearest seat, like an old lady afraid of breaking something. I feel so ashamed, and I don't know why. And why Brad Whitlock, the popular guy who had never before even bothered to acknowledge my existence all these years at Arkin High? I keep my eyes fixed on the landscape and concentrate on keeping them dry.

As soon as the bus doors open at school, I rush out without looking back. Once I join the tide of people flowing into the brick building, my heartbeat finally starts to settle. Now I feel protected, anonymous. Inside, excited voices unite in a single deafening roar, punctuated by the staccato of slamming locker doors.

"Hey, Ellen!" Jessie's voice rises above the din. She will never know how glad I am to see her familiar face.

"Hi, Jess!" I say, keeping a falsetto of cheerfulness on my voice.

"Are you okay?" Jessie's big brown eyes study me closely. Then the prefinal bell rings.

"I'm fine, thanks, Jess." I slam our locker door, imagining that Brad Whitlock's fingers are caught in it.

Maybe someday I'll stop to really think about it, about what it means to be different.

The prefinal bell means that I have one minute to get to room 2-D, the chemistry classroom. I see my friend Beth sitting in the corner by the window. I also see Tomper Sandel—all muscles under his Arkin High Football T-shirt—sitting in the same row.

Crossing the room to join Beth, I pass Tomper's desk.

"Hi, Ellen," he says, and smiles.

"Uh, hi Tomper," I say, trying not to stare. Tomper Sandel—saying hi to me?

"Ahem," says Mr. Borglund, our teacher, as he stands in front of the class. He looks like a cartoon character: his skin is as dark and wrinkled as a dried apple, and his hair-which I'm sure was blond in his younger years—stands straight and stiff, the color of a Brillo Pad, on top of his head.

When he tells us to pick lab partners, Beth and I quickly choose each other. Mr. Borglund ushers us all across the hall to the lab room, which has rows of black counters with sinks and weird spigots crusted with powdery precipitates of experiments past.

"Chemistry is based on the metric system," Mr. Borglund says to us. "For instance, instead of pounds, we have grams. There are 454 grams to a pound. Familiarize yourselves with the meter sticks, scales, and graduates in your lab kits. Then do the problems I'm handing out."

Beth and I dig out the tangled mess of beakers, scales, and rulers from our lab cubby. Beth starts balancing her plastic bracelet against the tiny gram weights, which look like metal Monopoly pieces.

"How was your summer?" she asks.

"Pretty good," I say. "Are you going out for gymnastics again?"

"For sure," she says. "You are, aren't you?"

"I'm planning on it," I say, thinking how Mom and Father had cautioned me that if any of my grades fell lower than an A, there would be no more gymnastics.

Mr. Borglund has given us three problems on converting from the U.S. to the metric system. It's almost too easy: once you know the formula, it's the same for all three. Beth works it out on her calculator, and I double-check the numbers to make sure they are absolutely right. Then I hand in the paper, after writing ELLEN SUNG and BETH ZEIGLER neatly at the top. We are the first group to finish. The two guys sharing our counter are fencing with their meter sticks.

We are putting the equipment away when Tomper pokes his head into our lab space.

"How's it going over here?" he asks. I look at him warily, but thrill at his faint smell of smoke; it reminds me of log cabins and chopping wood.

"We're just finishing up," Beth chirps. I give Beth a look to let her know that we'd better not give him any answers, since that's what he's probably here for.

"How's gymnastics going, Ellen?" He turns to me and grins, his chin folding into a perfect dimple—adorable.

"Our first meet is in a few weeks," I say, then add, "Beth is going out for it again, too."

"I'll be there," he says, giving the thumbs-up sign and smiling right into my face.

He walks away, hands casually thrust into the pockets of his faded Levi's. From the back, his gold hair curls down his tanned neck. What luck to finally have him in a class.

"He's gorgeous." Beth sighs.

"Too flirtatious," I say as coolly as I can.

English composition is the last class of the day. My interest perks up when I see Tomper Sandel walk in the door ahead of me.

I take a seat next to Beth, and we look up expectantly at our new teacher, Mrs. Klatsen. This class is one of those silly ones that they make all the seniors take to make sure everyone can read and write when they leave Arkin High. At least I've heard that Mrs. K. is supposed to be a good teacher.

Neatly stacked in front of her are *The Red Pony*, *The Good Earth*, *Tess of the d'Urbervilles*, and *The Complete Shakespeare*.

"Good books like these can open up worlds," she says, standing up regally. She must be at least six feet tall.

"Why not wait until the movie comes out?" calls Mike Anderson from the back of the room.

I look up at Mrs. K. She is smiling.

"Movies and TV are definitely entertaining," she says, not missing a beat. "But did you ever stop to think about how one-track they are? Movies and TV give you an entire picture and tell you exactly how to feel—they have the scary music and the canned laughter to make sure you get it right. But books, on the other hand, give you only the words; you have to use your imagination for the rest. It's more than entertainment: your imagination will help you get things from books that you'll carry with you for the rest of your life."

I look at Mike; his mouth is closed.

"For today, I'd like to see how well your vocabularies have held up over the summer. Pick your partner by writing down your first and second choice on a piece of paper."

How democratic, I think as I join the scribbling and scrabbling of pens. I write down BETH ZEIGLER, and then, as an afterthought, I put TOM SANDEL under her name. I tear the page out of my spiral-bound notebook and make sure it is folded up before I send it forward.

Mrs. K. sorts through the ragged papers and comes up with a list. Then she calls me to her desk.

"Ellen." Her eyes smile through her huge plastic glasses that make her look appealingly bookish. "Your last year's teacher, Mrs. Jaynes, told me about what a wonderful English student you are."

I try to smile modestly. It's true that English has always been one of my favorite classes.

"And a lot of people put you down for first choice."

Everyone knows I'm good with vocab words. I sigh to myself. *It's not like I'm popular or anything.*

"Whom did Beth put down?" I ask.

"Well, I thought that instead of Beth, I'd like to pair you with someone who needs a little help, and I wanted to make sure it was okay with you."

"Sure," I say hopefully. Maybe it'll be Tomper.

"I think," she says, "that Mike Anderson could benefit greatly from working with you."

I immediately think of Mike guffawing with Brad Whitlock at the bus stop this morning. Then Mrs. K. smiles such a straightforward, honest smile that I can't say anything. I like her too much.

So, Mike Anderson, the star hockey player with less-than-stellar brains, slides his desk along the floor like a scooter—until it bumps into mine.

"Hey, Ellen, how's life?" He grins suavely.

I pull out the vocab list, and his grin dissolves. "Ready?" I ask.

He rests his head on the desk and mumbles into his elbow, "Yeah."

The first word is *omniscient.*

"How about if we say 'God is considered to be omniscient'?"

"Yeah, sure," comes the muffled reply.

"Omniscient means all-knowing," I tell him for his benefit.

I do the next few words without seeing any signs of life from Mike.

"Here, you do the next one." I poke the pen into his hand, and he clambers out of his stupor with gruff surprise.

The word is *sentimental.*

He scratches his head for moment, looks at the word,

then looks at me. He seems so uncertain that I feel sorry for him. Don't they ever use *sentimental* in *Sports Illustrated*?

"Uh, how about 'They took a sentimental journey to the center of the earth'?" He beams. "Howzat?"

He might be popular, I'm thinking, *but he's sure not much to look at in the I.Q. department.*

Of course, when it is time to read the results out loud, we are called on for *sentimental.*

"It's your word," I murmur, giving him a nudge.

"Uh, sentimental. 'They took a sentimental journey to the center of the earth.'"

A pause. Then the class hoots with laughter. Even Mrs. Klatsen chuckles. Mike looks around and grins as if he planned to be funny.

That's what being popular is like—everyone thinks you're great no matter what you do.

"That's not quite it, Mike," she says. "Beth, you try."

"We became very sentimental when we heard our class song," she dutifully replies.

"Perfect," says Mrs. K.

I can't help wondering if Jessie's day is going any better. This is supposed to be our best year ever, she told me over the summer. A best year for best friends.

It is dinner time at the Sung household, and although she's absent, the presence of my sister still dominates.

"She was very disciplined," Father says as he begins

slurping at his Korean soup. "Even when she was getting all A's she still studied hard because she knew that being at the top of her class in a public school like Arkin wouldn't guarantee her getting into Harvard."

I tense my back against my chair. What good will it do for everyone to keep parading all of Michelle's accomplishments in front of me? Today in calculus class, Mr. Carlson, the teacher, delightedly shambled over when he saw me. "How's Michelle doing?" was the first thing that popped out of his mouth. "Boy, she was a whiz at math," was the second. I sat there wondering if he knew what my name was.

I look down at my lasagna. Its tomatoey garlicky smell mingles with the smell of seaweed from Father's soup. Since Mom has always cooked something Korean for Father and something "American" for her, Michelle, and me, the smells are always clashing, usually ending up in weird, cloying odors.

"How was school today?" Mom asks.

"Okay. Not much new," I say, although there's so much I want to say, that I wish I could say, that I can't.

I mentally close my eyes and envision a different conversation.

"A boy called me a 'chink' on the bus today," I would say. Mom's mouth would open. Father's chopsticks would drop, sinking unnoticed into the murky depths of his soup.

"You poor thing," Mom would say. "What did you do?"

"I totally ignored him," I would answer confidently.

"How terrible to have to go through that," Father would say, and he'd take off his thick spectacles so that for once I could see the tenderness in his eyes.

"With all this stress I think Ellen should worry less about grades and more about having a fun senior year and making friends," Mom would add.

"I agree," Father would say, and he'd resume slurping down his soup. *Slurp, slurp.*

"Ellen, why are you staring at your food?" I look at Mom. Father is slurping away, his head close to the bowl, the chopsticks poling all sorts of seaweed and bits of fish into his mouth.

"Just spacing out, Mom," I say.

"Did you find out about the language department?" Father asks between slurps.

"Yes." I know I've told him this before. "The school has canceled classes starting this year because they can't get enough kids in it."

"Remember to make it clear on your school applications that you only had three years of French because of a fault of the school's, not your own," he says.

"Yes, Father." I stare at the curly lasagna noodles again. College applications have been slowly advancing, like a storm gathering speed. What's going to happen to me? Michelle was a genius, a high school hermit who studied her brains out. I don't even know if I want to go halfway across the country for college.

After dinner, I troop up to my room to study. I know most kids have to help with the dishes, and I do feel a little guilty leaving Mom with the crusty lasagna pan and the big pot of stuff that looks as though it's been scooped up from a pond—but Mom and Father insist that my studies come first.

As I spread out my books, I leave my Holstein clock prominently in view, so I'll know to call Jessie at 8:00, as I usually do.

from Maizon at Blue Hill

Jacqueline Woodson

"It's cool tonight," Sandy whispered into the darkness.

I lay in my bed across from her, feeling strange. I have never shared a room with anyone but Margaret. "Yeah," I said. "It is."

Sandy was shorter than I was, but already she had started growing in places my body didn't even know existed. I had tried not to watch her getting dressed for bed, but couldn't help looking over when she was pulling her T-shirt on. She wasn't flat-chested like me. Her skin was so white I could see the blue veins running along her arms. There was hair under her arms.

"But the air coming in feels nice," I said.

"It does."

We lay silently across from each other for a while and I wondered if Sandy was as aware of my breathing as I was of hers. She breathed in and out slowly. Every now and then, she sighed.

I closed my eyes and tried to imagine Margaret lying across from me. But it didn't work. If it had been Margaret in the room, we would have climbed into the same bed hours ago and now we'd be gossiping and giggling and tickling each other until we cried.

I didn't like sharing with strangers.

"You have brothers and sisters, Maizon?" Sandy asked.

"Nope," I said, annoyed that she had broken through my thoughts. "Just me."

"Sometimes I wish I was an only child. I have two older sisters and two younger brothers," she confided.

"Middle child."

"I guess."

"Are they all in boarding school?"

In the darkness, I could see the shadow of Sandy raising up on her elbow. "Nope, just me. Blue Hill gave me a track scholarship disguised as an academic one."

"I didn't know you were on scholarship. I thought I was the only one."

"Are you kidding? Last year Blue Hill gave out fifty-four academic scholarships. Diana Cortez has one. She's a junior. So do my friends Sonia Chan and Gayle Childs—and Sara Carmona is on scholarship. But they're on different ones than me. Mine isn't for grades. I did lousy in grade school. But I made All-State in the quarter mile and I led my softball team to the championships. The paper wrote articles about me. You play sports?"

"Not really."

"You look like you'd be good in basketball. You're so tall and thin."

I felt a flicker of warmth toward Sandy. I had only been called "skinny," never "thin."

"I'm not coordinated. I mean, sometimes I am, but not a lot. Plus, I don't think I'd be good at team sports. I'm sort of an individual."

"That's 'cause you're an only child. My *family* is a team sport. I mean, there're so many of us." Sandy lay back down.

My mind was spinning a little bit. I hadn't even thought that Sandy was on scholarship. I knew I hadn't thought about it because she was white and I just figured that no white people would need help paying for Blue Hill. A long time ago, Ms. Dell had sat me and Margaret down in her kitchen with bowls of her famous Jell-O with cherries in front of us.

"You're gonna learn about racism and death and pain before you're teenagers," she warned. Margaret and I had nodded. By then we knew Ms. Dell had the gift to see into the future. "I'm gonna tell you this," Ms. Dell continued. "Racism doesn't know color, death doesn't know age, and pain doesn't know might."

Lying there, I wondered if it was racist of me to think all white people were rich.

Sandy's breathing slowed. After a while, when I couldn't hear it at all, I knew she was asleep.

I lay awake for a long time. What was it that made white people strange to me, that made Charli and Sheila and Marie seem threatening and safe at the same time? Why hadn't I asked myself these questions before?

"Because you never had to," I heard Ms. Dell murmur somewhere between my waking and sleeping.

Mr. Parsons hadn't lied about small classes. There were only twelve girls in my math class, eight in science, eight in French, nine in geography, and fourteen girls in my last class of the day, English. English class met in Laremy Hall, the gabled building I could see from my dorm window. It was right next to the main hall. We sat in a semicircle on the hardwood floor. Our teacher, Mrs. Dexter, wore a poncho and her hair cut short. She sat cross-legged at the opening of the circle. After we had gone around and introduced ourselves, Mrs. Dexter started talking. We would be doing Shakespeare this year, she promised. The class groaned. I hated the little bit of Shakespeare I had read.

"What's all the groaning?" Mrs. Dexter asked, smiling.

The class was silent.

"Can't he get his point across in fewer words?" I asked.

The class laughed. Some girls nodded.

For the next half hour we discussed what we'd be reading—*The Lottery*, *Animal Farm*, *A Light in the Forest*, *A*

Separate Peace, and a bunch of other books I hadn't heard of. But other girls in the class seemed to know everything about every book already. I listened to them, embarrassed that I had nothing to contribute, promising myself I'd start in on those books the minute I had a chance.

Then Mrs. Dexter asked us to choose a book we'd like to read in class. Everyone named their favorite book. Mrs. Dexter said some books people suggested were too easy. They got the ax.

"What about you, Maizon?"

I thought for a moment, feeling everyone's eyes on me. "I read a book last summer called *The Bluest Eye*, by a woman named Toni Morrison. I'd want to read that again."

Mrs. Dexter nodded. "That's a marvelous book," she said, and I felt myself grow warm. She wrote our suggestions down on a stray piece of looseleaf paper.

"We're going to start with your suggestions," she said to the class. "Then we'll do my reading."

The class groaned again, but underneath the complaining I could feel everybody's excitement, especially my own. I couldn't wait to reread *The Bluest Eye*.

After English, I made my way back to the main hall for the debate meeting. Some of the cross-country team were already doing half-mile sprints on the field. I watched them for a moment, wondering why anyone got a thrill running back and forth. Running only made me tired. Charli rushed by in her field hockey skirt.

"Miss Norman said to tell you to come by tomorrow if you have any interest in playing junior varsity."

I nodded.

"I help her coach them sometimes," Charli called, taking off into a jog. She lifted her shades and winked. "They're *so* cute and tiny," she mocked. I rolled my eyes. I hated being the youngest person, anywhere.

"Hey, Maizon!" Sybil said, opening the door and stepping back to allow me to enter. The room was a corner one, surrounded by windows and covered with dark blue carpeting. The windows let in a lot of sun. There were pictures of explorers on the wall. Chairs were set up in a semicircle the way they had been in all of my classes, except English, where there were no chairs. As I stood in front of one to peel my knapsack from my shoulders, the rest of the girls in the circle stared at me.

"Hi," I said softly, feeling strange. "Hi, everybody."

"Hey, Maizon," different people murmured. I recognized a few of the faces from different classes, but only knew two or three names.

"We've been talking about some of the issues we're going to be debating this year," Sybil said brightly. "But now, I guess, since this is everyone, I hope, we should give our names and stuff before we go on."

I nodded, figuring she was leading the group.

"I'm Maizon," I said, nodding toward the circle. "I'm a lower school freshman."

The group murmured a hello and similar introductions followed.

"You're the only freshman, Maizon," Sybil said, after all the introductions had been made.

"I'm used to being the only someone," I said.

The other girls laughed uneasily. I shrugged. The room suddenly felt hot to me and I pulled my collar away from my neck a little and pushed the sleeves of my blouse up to my elbows. Everyone watched this.

"How does it feel?" someone asked me, a girl whose name I didn't remember.

I shrugged again. "I haven't really thought about it much."

"I'd be interested in knowing what it's like here, actually . . ." Sybil said. "I mean, for you."

I said, "I'd be interested in knowing what it's like for *you*."

Sybil gave a quick look around the room and pulled her shoulders to her ears. "I don't think that would be too interesting," she said.

"Why not?"

"'Cause for me, it's the same as it is for everybody, I guess. Except you and Charli and them," she said.

"How do you know how it is for me?" The room was still. Heads had stopped moving from me to Sybil then back again and had dropped. The others listened without making their listening seem obvious. They were the heart of our conversation, the edges and the middle of it. "I mean, you and I have never even talked to each other, Sybil. That's why I want to know what it's like for you, and then I can see if it's the same for me."

Sybil looked up at me, her small dark eyes moving from one place on my face to another without meeting mine. "You know why it's different for you, Maizon," she said.

"I don't," I said, crossing my legs and leaning toward her. "I *am* smart, but I don't know everything. What makes Blue Hill so different for me?"

Someone coughed. I looked over at her and she covered her mouth with her hand.

I stared hard into Sybil's eyes, all the while knowing that what I was doing was wrong of me. What I saw there was Sybil's own fear of me and this made me madder than I had ever been. She had no right to have such a fear. She had never met me before, had never spoken to me or sat down beside me at dinner. It was the same fear that was in all of their eyes, but Sybil was the bravest. She was in charge and had chosen to raise her eyes and show me the fear there. I hated them all. But because she was brave, I hated Sybil the most.

"What's different?" I asked, giving a quick look around to include the others in this question. "I can't see me now, so you have to tell me, Sybil. What's so *different* about me?"

"You're black, Maizon," Sybil said. There was a near-silent longing in the back of her voice. I heard her desire, if only for a moment, an hour or a day, to be who I am. In Sybil's voice I heard the part of her—of each of them sitting in the room—who had always wanted to be the special one. The one like no other, who stands out and above only because she is allowed to, only because others have chosen to shrink in her presence.

I brushed at my skirt with my hand like I was flicking lint away, but it was really the moment I was ridding myself of. I thought of Marie and how she had brushed her thigh in the same way the first day we met. I was brushing away all of them with a flick of my hand. I felt the room shrink back away from me, felt their individual disappointment and felt the new strength of this power I had discovered within myself. "Yes, I am," I said, bringing the back of my hand to my eyes as though I were checking for the first time. "I am black, aren't I?"

No one said a word. I listened as someone called the meeting to order. It moved on slowly. I felt the other girls stealing glances at me. I felt mean all of a sudden. As they discussed the coming debates, my skirt had all of my attention. I stared at the dark green pleats riding along the front, at my skinny brown legs beneath it. I raised my feet in front of me and stared at my penny loafers, folded my arms across my chest, exhaled loudly to show my boredom and gazed at the starched, white creases in the sleeves of my blouse.

It seemed like hours before Sybil adjourned the meeting.

Only then, with the exits of the others, did the air in the room seem to lift.

"I hope we'll be friends, Maizon," Sybil said, when only she and I were left.

"Yeah. I hope so too." But the lie rode freely on the words, and Sybil knew it.

REVELATION

FLANNERY O'CONNOR

The doctor's waiting room, which was very small, was almost full when the Turpins entered and Mrs. Turpin, who was very large, made it look even smaller by her presence. She stood looming at the head of the magazine table set in the center of it, a living demonstration that the room was inadequate and ridiculous. Her little bright black eyes took in all the patients as she sized up the seating situation. There was one vacant chair and a place on the sofa occupied by a blond child in a dirty blue romper who should have been told to move over and make room for the lady. He was five or six, but Mrs. Turpin saw at once that no one was going to tell him to move over. He was slumped down in the seat, his arms idle at his sides and his eyes idle in his head; his nose ran unchecked.

Mrs. Turpin put a firm hand on Claud's shoulder and said in a voice that included anyone who wanted to listen, "Claud, you sit in that chair there," and gave him a push down into the vacant one. Claud was florid and bald and sturdy, somewhat shorter than Mrs. Turpin, but he sat down as if he were accustomed to doing what she told him to.

Mrs. Turpin remained standing. The only man in the room besides Claud was a lean stringy old fellow with a rusty hand spread out on each knee, whose eyes were closed as if he were asleep or dead or pretending to be so as not to get up and offer her his seat. Her gaze settled agreeably on a well-dressed grey-haired lady whose eyes met hers and whose expression said: if that child belonged to me, he would have some manners and move over—there's plenty of room there for you and him too.

Claud looked up with a sigh and made as if to rise.

"Sit down," Mrs. Turpin said. "You know you're not supposed to stand on that leg. He has an ulcer on his leg," she explained.

Claud lifted his foot onto the magazine table and rolled his trouser leg up to reveal a purple swelling on a plump marble-white calf.

"My!" the pleasant lady said. "How did you do that?"

"A cow kicked him," Mrs. Turpin said.

"Goodness!" said the lady.

Claud rolled his trouser leg down.

"Maybe the little boy would move over," the lady suggested, but the child did not stir.

"Somebody will be leaving in a minute," Mrs. Turpin said. She could not understand why a doctor—with as much money as they made charging five dollars a day to just stick their head in the hospital door and look at you—couldn't afford a decent-sized waiting room. This one was hardly bigger than a garage. The table was cluttered with limp-looking magazines and at one end of it there was a big green glass ash tray full of cigaret butts and cotton wads with little blood spots on them. If she had had anything to do with the running of the place, that would have been emptied every so often. There were no chairs against the wall at the head of the room. It had a rectangular-shaped panel in it that permitted a view of the office where the nurse came and went and the secretary listened to the radio. A plastic fern in a gold pot sat in the opening and trailed its fronds down almost to the floor. The radio was softly playing gospel music.

Just then the inner door opened and a nurse with the highest stack of yellow hair Mrs. Turpin had ever seen put her face in the crack and called for the next patient. The woman sitting beside Claud grasped the two arms of her chair and hoisted herself up; she pulled her dress free from her legs and lumbered through the door where the nurse had disappeared.

Mrs. Turpin eased into the vacant chair, which held her

tight as a corset. "I wish I could reduce," she said, and rolled her eyes and gave a comic sigh.

"Oh, *you* aren't fat," the stylish lady said.

"Ooooo I am too," Mrs. Turpin said. "Claud he eats all he wants to and never weighs over one hundred and seventy-five pounds, but me I just look at something good to eat and I gain some weight," and her stomach and shoulders shook with laughter. "You can eat all you want to, can't you, Claud?" she asked, turning to him.

Claud only grinned.

"Well, as long as you have such a good disposition," the stylish lady said, "I don't think it makes a bit of difference what size you are. You just can't beat a good disposition."

Next to her was a fat girl of eighteen or nineteen, scowling into a thick blue book which Mrs. Turpin saw was entitled *Human Development*. The girl raised her head and directed her scowl at Mrs. Turpin as if she did not like her looks. She appeared annoyed that anyone should speak while she tried to read. The poor girl's face was blue with acne and Mrs. Turpin thought how pitiful it was to have a face like that at that age. She gave the girl a friendly smile but the girl only scowled the harder. Mrs. Turpin herself was fat but she had always had good skin, and, though she was forty-seven years old, there was not a wrinkle in her face except around her eyes from laughing too much.

Next to the ugly girl was the child, still in exactly the same position, and next to him was a thin leathery old woman in a cotton print dress. She and Claud had three sacks of chicken feed in their pump house that was in the same print. She had seen from the first that the child belonged with the old woman. She could tell by the way they sat—kind of vacant and white-trashy, as if they would sit there until Doomsday if nobody called and told them to get up. And at right angles but next to the well-dressed pleasant lady was a lank-faced woman who was certainly the child's mother. She had on a yellow sweat shirt and wine-colored slacks, both gritty-looking, and the rims of her lips were stained with snuff. Her dirty yellow hair was tied behind with a little piece of red paper ribbon. Worse than niggers any day, Mrs. Turpin thought.

The gospel hymn playing was, "When I looked up and He looked down," and Mrs. Turpin, who knew it, supplied the last line mentally, "And wona these days I know I'll we-eara crown."

Without appearing to, Mrs. Turpin always noticed people's feet. The well-dressed lady had on red and grey suede shoes to match her dress. Mrs. Turpin had on her good black patent leather pumps. The ugly girl had on Girl Scout shoes and heavy socks. The old woman had on tennis shoes and the white-trashy mother had on what appeared to be bedroom slippers, black straw with gold braid threaded through them—exactly what you would have expected her to have on.

Sometimes at night when she couldn't go to sleep, Mrs. Turpin would occupy herself with the question of who she would have chosen to be if she couldn't have been herself. If Jesus had said to her before he made her, "There's only two places available for you. You can either be a nigger or white-trash," what would she have said? "Please, Jesus, please," she would have said, "just let me wait until there's another place available," and he would have said, "No, you have to go right now and I have only those two places so make up your mind." She would have wiggled and squirmed and begged and pleaded but it would have been no use and finally she would have said, "All right, make me a nigger then—but that don't mean a trashy one." And he would have made her a neat clean respectable Negro woman, herself but black.

Next to the child's mother was a red-headed youngish woman, reading one of the magazines and working a piece of chewing gum, hell for leather, as Claud would say. Mrs. Turpin could not see the woman's feet. She was not white-trash, just common. Sometimes Mrs. Turpin occupied herself at night naming the classes of people. On the bottom of the heap were most colored people, not the kind she would have been if she had been one, but most of them; then next to them—not above, just away from—were the white-trash; then above them were the home-owners, and above them the home-and-land owners, to which she and Claud belonged. Above she and Claud were people with a lot of money and much bigger houses and much more land. But here the complexity of it would begin to bear in on her, for some of the people with a lot of money were common and ought to be below she and Claud and some of the people who had good blood had lost their money and had to rent and then there were colored people who owned their homes and land as well. There was a colored dentist in town who had two red Lincolns and a swimming pool and a farm with registered white-face cattle on it. Usually by the time she had fallen asleep all the classes of people were moiling and roiling around in her head, and she would dream they were all crammed in together in a box car, being ridden off to be put in a gas oven.

"That's a beautiful clock," she said and nodded to her right. It was a big wall clock, the face encased in a brass sunburst.

"Yes, it's very pretty," the stylist lady said agreeably. "And right on the dot too," she added, glancing at her watch.

The ugly girl beside her cast an eye upward at the clock, smirked, then looked directly at Mrs. Turpin and smirked again. Then she returned her eyes to her book. She was obviously the lady's daughter because, although they didn't look anything alike as to disposition, they both had the same shape of face and the same blue eyes. On the lady they sparkled pleasantly but in the girl's seared face they appeared alternately to smolder and to blaze.

What if Jesus had said, "All right, you can be white-trash or a nigger or ugly"!

Mrs. Turpin felt an awful pity for the girl, though she thought it was one thing to be ugly and another to act ugly.

The woman with the snuff-stained lips turned around in her chair and looked up at the clock. Then she turned back and appeared to look a little to the side of Mrs. Turpin. There was a cast in one of her eyes. "You want to know wher you can get you one of themther clocks?" she asked in a loud voice.

"No, I already have a nice clock," Mrs. Turpin said. Once somebody like her got a leg in the conversation, she would be all over it.

"You can get you one with green stamps," the woman said. "That's most likely wher he got hisn. Save you up enough, you can get you most anythang. I got me some joo'ry."

Ought to have got you a wash rag and some soap, Mrs. Turpin thought.

"I get contour sheets with mine," the pleasant lady said.

The daughter slammed her book shut. She looked straight in front of her, directly through Mrs. Turpin and on through the yellow curtain and the plate glass window which made the wall behind her. The girl's eyes seemed lit all of a sudden with a peculiar light, an unnatural light like night road signs give. Mrs. Turpin turned her head to see if there was anything going on outside that she should see, but she could not see anything. Figures passing cast only a pale shadow through the curtain. There was no reason the girl should single her out for her ugly looks.

"Miss Finley," the nurse said, cracking the door. The

gum-chewing woman got up and passed in front of her and Claud and went into the office. She had on red high-heeled shoes.

Directly across the table, the ugly girl's eyes were fixed on Mrs. Turpin as if she had some very special reason for disliking her.

"This is wonderful weather, isn't it?" the girl's mother said.

"It's good weather for cotton if you can get the niggers to pick it," Mrs. Turpin said, "but niggers don't want to pick cotton any more. You can't get the white folks to pick it and now you can't get the niggers—because they got to be right up there with the white folks."

"They gonna *try* anyways," the white-trash woman said, leaning forward.

"Do you have one of those cotton-picking machines?" the pleasant lady asked.

"No," Mrs. Turpin said, "they leave half the cotton in the field. We don't have much cotton anyway. If you want to make it farming now, you have to have a little of everything. We got a couple of acres of cotton and a few hogs and chickens and just enough white-face that Claud can look after them himself."

"One thang I don't want," the white-trash woman said, wiping her mouth with the back of her hand. "Hogs. Nasty stinking things, a-gruntin and a-rootin all over the place."

Mrs. Turpin gave her the merest edge of her attention. "Our hogs are not dirty and they don't stink," she said.

"They're cleaner than some children I've seen. Their feet never touch the ground. We have a pig parlor—that's where you raise them on concrete," she explained to the pleasant lady, "and Claud scoots them down with the hose every afternoon and washes off the floor." Cleaner by far than that child right there, she thought. Poor nasty little thing. He had not moved except to put the thumb of his dirty hand into his mouth.

The woman turned her face away from Mrs. Turpin. "I know I wouldn't scoot down no hog with no hose," she said to the wall.

You wouldn't have no hog to scoot down, Mrs. Turpin said to herself.

"A-gruntin and a-rootin and a-groanin," the woman muttered.

"We got a little of everything," Mrs. Turpin said to the pleasant lady. "It's no use in having more than you can handle yourself with help like it is. We found enough niggers to pick our cotton this year but Claud he has to go after them and take them home again in the evening. They can't walk that half a mile. No they can't. I tell you," she said and laughed merrily, "I sure am tired of buttering up niggers, but you got to love em if you want em to work for you. When they come in the morning, I run out and I say, 'Hi yawl this morning?' and when Claud drives them off to the field I just wave to beat the band and they just wave back." And she waved her hand rapidly to illustrate.

"Like you read out of the same book," the lady said, showing she understood perfectly.

"Child, yes," Mrs. Turpin said. "And when they come in from the field, I run out with a bucket of icewater. That's the way it's going to be from now on," she said. "You may as well face it."

"One thang I know," the white-trash woman said. "Two thangs I ain't going to do: love no niggers or scoot down no hog with no hose." And she let out a bark of contempt.

The look that Mrs. Turpin and the pleasant lady exchanged indicated they both understood that you had to *have* certain things before you could *know* certain things. But every time Mrs. Turpin exchanged a look with the lady, she was aware that the ugly girl's peculiar eyes were still on her, and she had trouble bringing her attention back to the conversation.

"When you got something," she said, "you got to look after it." And when you ain't got a thing but breath and britches, she added to herself, you can afford to come to town every morning and just sit on the Court House coping and spit.

A grotesque revolving shadow passed across the curtain behind her and was thrown palely on the opposite wall. Then a bicycle clattered down against the outside of the building. The door opened and a colored boy glided in with a tray from the drug store. It had two large red and white paper cups on it with tops on them. He was a tall, very black boy in discolored white pants and a green nylon shirt. He was chewing gum slowly, as if to music. He set the tray down in the office opening next to the fern and stuck his head through to look for the secretary. She was not in there. He rested his arms on the ledge and waited, his narrow bottom stuck out, swaying slowly to the left and right. He raised a hand over his head and scratched the base of his skull.

"You see that button there, boy?" Mrs. Turpin said. "You can punch that and she'll come. She's probably in the back somewhere."

"Is that right?" the boy said agreeably, as if he had never seen the button before. He leaned to the right and put his finger on it. "She sometime out," he said and twisted around to face his audience, his elbows behind him on the counter. The nurse appeared and he twisted back again. She handed him a dollar and he rooted in his pocket and made the change and counted it out to her. She gave him fifteen cents for a tip and he went out with the empty tray. The heavy door swung to slowly and closed at length with the sound of suction. For a moment no one spoke.

"They ought to send all them niggers back to Africa," the white-trash woman said. "That's wher they come from in the first place."

"Oh, I couldn't do without my good colored friends," the pleasant lady said.

"There's a heap of things worse than a nigger," Mrs.

Turpin agreed. "It's all kinds of them just like it's all kinds of us."

"Yes, and it takes all kinds to make the world go round," the lady said in her musical voice.

As she said it, the raw-complexioned girl snapped her teeth together. Her lower lip turned downwards and inside out, revealing the pale pink inside of her mouth. After a second it rolled back up. It was the ugliest face Mrs. Turpin had ever seen anyone make and for a moment she was certain that the girl had made it at her. She was looking at her as if she had known and disliked her all her life—all of Mrs. Turpin's life, it seemed too, not just all the girl's life. Why, girl, I don't even know you, Mrs. Turpin said silently.

She forced her attention back to the discussion. "It wouldn't be practical to send them back to Africa," she said. "They wouldn't want to go. They got it too good here."

"Wouldn't be what they wanted—if I had anythang to do with it," the woman said.

"It wouldn't be a way in the world you could get all the niggers back over there," Mrs. Turpin said. "They'd be hiding out and lying down and turning sick on you and wailing and hollering and raring and pitching. It wouldn't be a way in the world to get them over there."

"They got over here," the trashy woman said. "Get back like they got over."

"It wasn't so many of them then," Mrs. Turpin explained.

The woman looked at Mrs. Turpin as if here was an idiot indeed but Mrs. Turpin was not bothered by the look, considering where it came from.

"Nooo," she said, "they're going to stay here where they can go to New York and marry white folks and improve their color. That's what they all want to do, every one of them, improve their color."

"You know what comes of that, don't you?" Claud asked.

"No, Claud, what?" Mrs. Turpin said.

Claud's eyes twinkled. "White-faced niggers," he said with never a smile.

Everybody in the office laughed except the white-trash and the ugly girl. The girl gripped the book in her lap with white fingers. The trashy woman looked around her from face to face as if she thought they were all idiots. The old woman in the feed sack dress continued to gaze expressionless across the floor at the high-top shoes of the man opposite her, the one who had been pretending to be asleep when the Turpins came in. He was laughing heartily, his hands still spread out on his knees. The child had fallen to the side and was lying now almost face down in the old woman's lap.

While they recovered from their laughter, the nasal chorus on the radio kept the room from silence.

You go to blank blank
And I'll go to mine

But we'll all blank along
To-geth-ther,
And all along the blank
We'll hep eachother out
Smile-ling in any kind of
Weath-ther!

Mrs. Turpin didn't catch every word but she caught enough to agree with the spirit of the song and it turned her thoughts sober. To help anybody out that needed it was her philosophy of life. She never spared herself when she found somebody in need, whether they were white or black, trash or decent. And of all she had to be thankful for, she was most thankful that this was so. If Jesus had said, "You can be high society and have all the money you want and be thin and svelte-like, but you can't be a good woman with it," she would have had to say, "Well don't make me that then. Make me a good woman and it don't matter what else, how fat or how ugly or how poor!" Her heart rose. He had not made her a nigger or white-trash or ugly! He had made her herself and given her a little of everything. Jesus, thank you! she said. Thank you thank you thank you! Whenever she counted her blessings she felt as buoyant as if she weighed one hundred and twenty-five pounds instead of one hundred and eighty.

"What's wrong with your little boy?" the pleasant lady asked the white-trashy woman.

"He has a ulcer," the woman said proudly. "He ain't

give me a minute's peace since he was born. Him and her are just alike," she said, nodding at the old woman, who was running her leathery fingers through the child's pale hair. "Look like I can't get nothing down them two but Co' Cola and candy."

That's all you try to get down em, Mrs. Turpin said to herself. Too lazy to light the fire. There was nothing you could tell her about people like them that she didn't know already. And it was not just that they didn't have anything. Because if you gave them everything, in two weeks it would all be broken or filthy or they would have chopped it up for lightwood. She knew all this from her own experience. Help them you must, but help them you couldn't.

All at once the ugly girl turned her lips inside out again. Her eyes were fixed like two drills on Mrs. Turpin. This time there was no mistaking that there was something urgent behind them.

Girl, Mrs. Turpin exclaimed silently, I haven't done a thing to you! The girl might be confusing her with somebody else. There was no need to sit by and let herself be intimidated. "You must be in college," she said boldly, looking directly at the girl. "I see you reading a book there."

The girl continued to stare and pointedly did not answer.

Her mother blushed at this rudeness. "The lady asked you a question, Mary Grace," she said under her breath.

"I have ears," Mary Grace said.

The poor mother blushed again. "Mary Grace goes to Wellesley College," she explained. She twisted one of the buttons on her dress. "In Massachusetts," she added with a grimace. "And in the summer she just keeps right on studying. Just reads all the time, a real book worm. She's done real well at Wellesley; she's taking English and Math and History and Psychology and Social Studies," she rattled on, "and I think it's too much. I think she ought to get out and have fun."

The girl looked as if she would like to hurl them all through the plate glass window.

"Way up north," Mrs. Turpin murmured and thought, well, it hasn't done much for her manners.

"I'd almost rather to have him sick," the white-trash woman said, wrenching the attention back to herself. "He's so mean when he ain't. Look like some children just take natural to meanness. It's some gets bad when they get sick but he was the opposite. Took sick and turned good. He don't give me no trouble now. It's me waitin to see the doctor," she said.

If I was going to send anybody back to Africa, Mrs. Turpin thought, it would be your kind, woman. "Yes, indeed," she said aloud, but looking up at the ceiling, "it's a heap of things worse than a nigger." And dirtier than a hog, she added to herself.

"I think people with bad dispositions are more to be pitied than anyone on earth," the pleasant lady said in a voice that was decidedly thin.

"I thank the Lord he has blessed me with a good one," Mrs. Turpin said. "The day has never dawned that I couldn't find something to laugh at."

"Not since she married me anyways," Claud said with a comical straight face.

Everybody laughed except the girl and the white-trash.

Mrs. Turpin's stomach shook. "He's such a caution," she said, "that I can't help but laugh at him."

The girl made a loud ugly noise through her teeth.

Her mother's mouth grew thin and tight. "I think the worst thing in the world," she said, "is an ungrateful person. To have everything and not appreciate it. I know a girl," she said, "who has parents who would give her anything, a little brother who loves her dearly, who is getting a good education, who wears the best clothes, but who can never say a kind word to anyone, who never smiles, who just criticizes and complains all day long."

"Is she too old to paddle?" Claud asked.

The girl's face was almost purple.

"Yes," the lady said, "I'm afraid there's nothing to do but leave her to her folly. Some day she'll wake up and it'll be too late."

"It never hurt anyone to smile," Mrs. Turpin said. "It just makes you feel better all over."

"Of course," the lady said sadly, "but there are just some people you can't tell anything to. They can't take criticism."

"If it's one thing I am," Mrs. Turpin said with feeling,

"it's grateful. When I think who all I could have been besides myself and what all I got, a little of everything, and a good disposition besides, I just feel like shouting, 'Thank you, Jesus, for making everything the way it is!' It could have been different!" For one thing, somebody else could have got Claud. At the thought of this, she was flooded with gratitude and a terrible pang of joy ran through her. "Oh thank you, Jesus, Jesus, thank you!" she cried aloud.

The book struck her directly over her left eye. It struck almost at the same instant that she realized the girl was about to hurl it. Before she could utter a sound, the raw face came crashing across the table toward her, howling. The girl's fingers sank like clamps into the soft flesh of her neck. She heard the mother cry out and Claud shout, "Whoa!" There was an instant when she was certain that she was about to be in an earthquake.

All at once her vision narrowed and she saw everything as if it were happening in a small room far away, or as if she were looking at it through the wrong end of a telescope. Claud's face crumpled and fell out of sight. The nurse ran in, then out, then in again. Then the gangling figure of the doctor rushed out of the inner door. Magazines flew this way and that as the table turned over. The girl fell with a thud and Mrs. Turpin's vision suddenly reversed itself and she saw everything large instead of small. The eyes of the white-trashy woman were staring hugely at the floor. There the girl, held down on one side by the nurse and on the other by her mother, was wrenching and turning in their grasp. The doctor was kneeling astride her, trying to hold her arm down. He managed after a second to sink a long needle into it.

Mrs. Turpin felt entirely hollow except for her heart which swung from side to side as if it were agitated in a great empty drum of flesh.

"Somebody that's not busy call for the ambulance," the doctor said in the off-hand voice young doctors adopt for terrible occasions.

Mrs. Turpin could not have moved a finger. The old man who had been sitting next to her skipped nimbly into the office and made the call, for the secretary still seemed to be gone.

"Claud!" Mrs. Turpin called.

He was not in his chair. She knew she must jump up and find him but she felt like some one trying to catch a train in a dream, when everything moves in slow motion and the faster you try to run the slower you go.

"Here I am," a suffocated voice, very unlike Claud's, said.

He was doubled up in the corner on the floor, pale as paper, holding his leg. She wanted to get up and go to him but she could not move. Instead, her gaze was drawn slowly downward to the churning face on the floor, which she could see over the doctor's shoulder.

The girl's eyes stopped rolling and focused on her. They seemed a much lighter blue than before, as if a door that had been tightly closed behind them was now open to admit light and air.

Mrs. Turpin's head cleared and her power of motion returned. She leaned forward until she was looking directly into the fierce brilliant eyes. There was no doubt in her mind that the girl did know her, knew her in some intense and personal way, beyond time and place and condition. "What you got to say to me?" she asked hoarsely and held her breath, waiting, as for a revelation.

The girl raised her head. Her gaze locked with Mrs. Turpin's. "Go back to hell where you came from, you old wart hog," she whispered. Her voice was low but clear. Her eyes burned for a moment as if she saw with pleasure that her message had struck its target.

Mrs. Turpin sank back in her chair.

After a moment the girl's eyes closed and she turned her head wearily to the side.

The doctor rose and handed the nurse the empty syringe. He leaned over and put both hands for a moment on the mother's shoulders, which were shaking. She was sitting on the floor, her lips pressed together, holding Mary Grace's hand in her lap. The girl's fingers were gripped like a baby's around her thumb. "Go on to the hospital," he said. "I'll call and make the arrangements."

"Now let's see that neck," he said in a jovial voice to Mrs. Turpin. He began to inspect her neck with his first two fingers. Two little moon-shaped lines like pink fish bones were indented over her windpipe. There was the beginning of an angry red swelling above her eye. His fingers passed over this also.

"Lea' me be," she said thickly and shook him off. "See about Claud. She kicked him."

"I'll see about him in a minute," he said and felt her pulse. He was a thin grey-haired man, given to pleasantries. "Go home and have yourself a vacation the rest of the day," he said and patted her on the shoulder.

Quit your pattin me, Mrs. Turpin growled to herself.

"And put an ice pack over that eye," he said. Then he went and squatted down beside Claud and looked at his leg. After a moment he pulled him up and Claud limped after him into the office.

Until the ambulance came, the only sounds in the room were the tremulous moans of the girl's mother, who continued to sit on the floor. The white-trash woman did not take her eyes off the girl. Mrs. Turpin looked straight ahead at nothing. Presently the ambulance drew up, a long dark shadow, behind the curtain. The attendants came and set the stretcher down beside the girl and lifted her expertly onto it and carried her out. The nurse helped the mother gather up her things. The shadow of the ambulance moved silently away and the nurse came back in the office.

"That ther girl is going to be a lunatic, ain't she?" the white-trash woman asked the nurse, but the nurse kept on to the back and never answered her.

"Yes, she's going to be a lunatic," the white-trash woman said to the rest of them.

"Po' critter," the old woman murmured. The child's face was still in her lap. His eyes looked idly out over her knees. He had not moved during the disturbance except to draw one leg up under him.

"I thank Gawd," the white-trash woman said fervently, "I ain't a lunatic."

Claud came limping out and the Turpins went home.

As their pick-up truck turned into their own dirt road and made the crest of the hill, Mrs. Turpin gripped the window ledge and looked out suspiciously. The land sloped gracefully down through a field dotted with lavender weeds and at the start of the rise their small yellow frame house, with its little flower beds spread out around it like a fancy apron, sat primly in its accustomed place between two giant hickory trees. She would not have been startled to see a burnt wound between two blackened chimneys.

Neither of them felt like eating so they put on their house clothes and lowered the shade in the bedroom and lay down, Claud with his leg on a pillow and herself with a damp washcloth over her eye. The instant she was flat on her back, the image of a razor-backed hog with warts on its face and horns coming out behind its ears snorted into her head. She moaned, a low quiet moan.

"I am not," she said tearfully, "a wart hog. From hell." But the denial had no force. The girl's eyes and her words, even the tone of her voice, low but clear, directed only to her, brooked no repudiation. She had been singled out for the message, though there was trash in the room to whom it might justly have been applied. The full force of this fact struck her only now. There was a woman there who was neglecting her own child but she had been overlooked. The message had been given to Ruby Turpin, a respectable, hard-working, church-going woman. The tears dried. Her eyes began to burn instead with wrath.

She rose on her elbow and the washcloth fell into her hand. Claud was lying on his back, snoring. She wanted to tell him what the girl had said. At the same time, she did not wish to put the image of herself as a wart hog from hell into his mind.

"Hey, Claud," she muttered and pushed his shoulder.

Claud opened one pale baby blue eye.

She looked into it warily. He did not think about anything. He just went his way.

"Wha, whasit?" he said and closed the eye again.

"Nothing," she said. "Does your leg pain you?"

"Hurts like hell," Claud said.

"It'll quit terreckly," she said and lay back down. In a moment Claud was snoring again. For the rest of the afternoon they lay there. Claud slept. She scowled at the ceiling. Occasionally she raised her fist and made a small stabbing motion over her chest as if she was defending her innocence to invisible guests who were like the comforters of Job, reasonable-seeming but wrong.

About five-thirty Claud stirred. "Got to go after those niggers," he sighed, not moving.

She was looking straight up as if there were unintelligible handwriting on the ceiling. The protuberance over her eye had turned a greenish-blue. "Listen here," she said.

"What?"

"Kiss me."

Claud leaned over and kissed her loudly on the mouth. He pinched her side and their hands interlocked. Her expression of ferocious concentration did not change. Claud got up, groaning and growling, and limped off. She continued to study the ceiling.

She did not get up until she heard the pick-up truck coming back with the Negroes. Then she rose and thrust her feet in her brown oxfords, which she did not bother to lace, and stumped out onto the back porch and got her red plastic bucket. She emptied a tray of ice cubes into it and filled it half full of water and went out into the back yard. Every afternoon after Claud brought the hands in, one of the boys helped him put out hay and the rest waited in the back of the truck until he was ready to take them home. The truck was parked in the shade under one of the hickory trees.

"Hi yawl this evening?" Mrs. Turpin asked grimly, appearing with the bucket and the dipper. There were three women and a boy in the truck.

"Us doin nicely," the oldest woman said. "Hi you doin?" and her gaze stuck immediately on the dark lump on Mrs. Turpin's forehead. "You done fell down, ain't you?" she asked in a solicitous voice. The old woman was dark and almost toothless. She had on an old felt hat of Claud's set back on her head. The other two women were younger and lighter and they both had new bright green sun hats. One of them had hers on her head; the other had taken hers off and the boy was grinning beneath it.

Mrs. Turpin set the bucket down on the floor of the truck. "Yawl hep yourselves," she said. She looked around to make sure Claud had gone. "No. I didn't fall down," she said, folding her arms. "It was something worse than that."

"Ain't nothing bad happen to you!" the old woman said. She said it as if they all knew that Mrs. Turpin was protected in some special way by Divine Providence. "You just had you a little fall."

"We were in town at the doctor's office for where the cow kicked Mr. Turpin," Mrs. Turpin said in a flat tone that indicated they could leave off their foolishness. "And there was this girl there. A big fat girl with her face all broke out. I could look at that girl and tell she was peculiar but I couldn't tell how. And me and her mama were just talking and going along and all of a sudden WHAM! She throws this big book she was reading at me and . . ."

"Naw!" the old woman cried out.

"And then she jumps over the table and commences to choke me."

"Naw!" they all exclaimed, "naw!"

"Hi come she do that?" the old woman asked. "What ail her?"

Mrs. Turpin only glared in front of her.

"Somethin ail her," the old woman said.

"They carried her off in an ambulance," Mrs. Turpin continued, "but before she went she was rolling on the floor and they were trying to hold her down to give her a shot and she said something to me." She paused. "You know what she said to me?"

"What she say?" they asked.

"She said," Mrs. Turpin began, and stopped, her face very dark and heavy. The sun was getting whiter and whiter, blanching the sky overhead so that the leaves of the hickory tree were black in the face of it. She could not bring forth the words. "Something real ugly," she muttered.

"She sho shouldn't said nothin ugly to you," the old woman said. "You so sweet. You the sweetest lady I know."

"She pretty too," the one with the hat on said.

"And stout," the other one said. "I never knowed no sweeter white lady."

"That's the truth befo' Jesus," the old woman said. "Amen! You des as sweet and pretty as you can be."

Mrs. Turpin knew just exactly how much Negro flattery was worth and it added to her rage. "She said," she began again and finished this time with a fierce rush of breath, "that I was an old wart hog from hell."

There was an astounded silence.

"Where she at?" the youngest woman cried in a piercing voice.

"Lemme see her. I'll kill her!"

"I'll kill her with you!" the other one cried.

"She b'long in the sylum," the old woman said emphatically. "You the sweetest white lady I know."

"She pretty too," the other two said. "Stout as she can be and sweet. Jesus satisfied with her!"

"Deed he is," the old woman declared.

Idiots! Mrs. Turpin growled to herself. You could never say anything intelligent to a nigger. You could talk at them but not with them. "Yawl ain't drunk your water," she said shortly. "Leave the bucket in the truck when you're finished with it. I got more to do than just stand around and pass the time of day," and she moved off and into the house.

She stood for a moment in the middle of the kitchen. The dark protuberance over her eye looked like a miniature tornado cloud which might any moment sweep across the horizon of her brow. Her lower lip protruded dangerously. She squared her massive shoulders. Then she marched into the front of the house and out the side door and started down the road to the pig parlor. She had the look of a woman going single-handed, weaponless, into battle.

The sun was deep yellow now like a harvest moon and

was riding westward very fast over the far tree line as if it meant to reach the hogs before she did. The road was rutted and she kicked several good-sized stones out of her path as she strode along. The pig parlor was on a little knoll at the end of a lane that ran off from the side of the barn. It was a square of concrete as large as a small room, with a board fence about four feet high around it. The concrete floor sloped slightly so that the hog wash could drain off into a trench where it was carried to the field for fertilizer. Claud was standing on the outside, on the edge of the concrete, hanging onto the top board, hosing down the floor inside. The hose was connected to the faucet of a water trough nearby.

Mrs. Turpin climbed up beside him and glowered down at the hogs inside. There were seven long-snouted bristly shoats in it—tan with liver-colored spots—and an old sow a few weeks off from farrowing. She was lying on her side grunting. The shoats were running about shaking themselves like idiot children, their little slit pig eyes searching the floor for anything left. She had read that pigs were the most intelligent animal. She doubted it. They were supposed to be smarter than dogs. There had even been a pig astronaut. He had performed his assignment perfectly but died of a heart attack afterwards because they left him in his electric suit, sitting upright throughout his examination when naturally a hog should be on all fours.

A-gruntin and a-rootin and a-groanin.

"Gimme that hose," she said, yanking it away from Claud. "Go on and carry them niggers home and get off that leg."

"You look like you might have swallowed a mad dog," Claud observed, but he got down and limped off. He paid no attention to her humors.

Until he was out of earshot, Mrs. Turpin stood on the side of the pen, holding the hose and pointing the stream of water at the hind quarters of any shoat that looked as if it might try to lie down. When he had had time to get over the hill, she turned her head slightly and her wrathful eyes scanned the path. He was nowhere in sight. She turned back again and seemed to gather herself up. Her shoulders rose and she drew in her breath.

"What do you send me a message like that for?" she said in a low fierce voice, barely above a whisper but with the force of a shout in its concentrated fury. "How am I a hog and me both? How am I saved and from hell too?" Her free fist was knotted and with the other she gripped the hose, blindly pointing the stream of water in and out of the eye of the old sow whose outraged squeal she did not hear.

The pig parlor commanded a view of the back pasture where their twenty beef cows were gathered around the hay bales Claud and the boy had put out. The freshly cut pasture sloped down to the highway. Across it was their cotton field and beyond that a dark green dusty wood which they owned as well. The sun was behind the wood, very red, looking over the paling of trees like a farmer inspecting his own hogs.

"Why me?" she rumbled. "It's no trash around here, black or white, that I haven't given to. And break my back to the bone every day working. And do for the church."

She appeared to be the right size woman to command the arena before her. "How am I a hog?" she demanded. "Exactly how am I like them?" and she jabbed the stream of water at the shoats. "There was plenty of trash there. It didn't have to be me.

"If you like trash better, go get yourself some trash then," she railed. "You could have made me trash. Or a nigger. If trash is what you wanted why didn't you make me trash?" She shook her fist with the hose in it and a watery snake appeared momentarily in the air. "I could quit working and take it easy and be filthy," she growled. "Lounge about the sidewalks all day drinking root beer. Dip snuff and spit in every puddle and have it all over my face. I could be nasty.

"Or you could have made me a nigger. It's too late for me to be a nigger," she said with deep sarcasm, "but I could act like one. Lay down in the middle of the road and stop traffic. Roll on the ground."

In the deepening light everything was taking on a mysterious hue. The pasture was growing a peculiar glassy green and the streak of highway had turned lavender. She braced herself for a final assault and this time her voice rolled out over the pasture. "Go on," she yelled, "call me a hog! Call me a hog again. From hell. Call me a wart hog from hell. Put that bottom rail on top. There'll still be a top and bottom!"

A garbled echo returned to her.

A final surge of fury shook her and she roared, "Who do you think you are?"

The color of everything, field and crimson sky, burned for a moment with a transparent intensity. The question carried over the pasture and across the highway and the cotton field and returned to her clearly like an answer from beyond the wood.

She opened her mouth but no sound came out of it.

A tiny truck, Claud's, appeared on the highway, heading rapidly out of sight. Its gears scraped thinly. It looked like a child's toy. At any moment a bigger truck might smash into it and scatter Claud's and the niggers' brains all over the road.

Mrs. Turpin stood there, her gaze fixed on the highway, all her muscles rigid, until in five or six minutes the truck reappeared, returning. She waited until it had had time to turn into their own road. Then like a monumental statue coming to life, she bent her head slowly and gazed, as if through the very heart of mystery, down into the pig parlor at the hogs. They had settled all in one corner around the old sow who was grunting softly. A red glow suffused them. They appeared to pant with a secret life.

Until the sun slipped finally behind the tree line, Mrs. Turpin remained there with her gaze bent to them as if she were absorbing some abysmal life-giving knowledge. At last she lifted her head. There was only a purple streak in the sky, cutting through a field of crimson and leading, like an extension of the highway, into the descending dusk. She raised her hands from the side of the pen in a gesture hieratic and profound. A visionary light settled in her eyes. She saw the streak as a vast swinging bridge extending upward from the earth through a field of living fire. Upon it a vast horde of souls were rumbling toward heaven. There were whole companies of white-trash, clean for the first time in their lives, and bands of black niggers in white robes, and battalions of freaks and lunatics shouting and clapping and leaping like frogs. And bringing up the end of the procession was a tribe of people whom she recognized at once as those who, like herself and Claud, had always had a little of everything and the God-given wit to use it right. She leaned forward to observe them closer. They were marching behind the others with great dignity, accountable as they had always been for good order and common sense and respectable behavior. They alone were on key. Yet she could see by their shocked and altered faces that even their virtues were being burned away. She lowered her hands and gripped the rail of the hog pen, her eyes small but fixed unblinkingly on what lay ahead. In a moment the vision faded but she remained where she was, immobile.

At length she got down and turned off the faucet and made her slow way on the darkening path to the house. In the woods around her the invisible cricket choruses had struck up, but what she heard were the voices of the souls climbing upward into the starry field and shouting hallelujah.

from Betsey Brown

Ntozake Shange

Jane had never been in and out of the refrigerator so much in her life. Nobody wanted anything they usually ate.

"I never eat baloney, Mama," Margot pouted.

"I do, I eat it all the time," Allard said.

"Y'all shut up, and get out my way. I've got to see if my bus is coming." Sharon pushed her way to the window, paper bag lunch in hand.

"You in that much of a hurry for the crackers[1] to spit on you?" Charlie asked.

"But, Mama, I don't like tuna." Margot still hadn't found a luncheon meat that satisfied her tastes. "I don't want cheese, either."

[1] poor, usually Southern whites; used disparagingly

Betsey was roaming among them like a prelate. "It's the law. Integration is the law."

Jane reached her limit.

"This is it. Here are your lunches. It's the law. Go to your bus stops and have a good day."

Greer lifted Allard off the floor to the ceiling and let him play Spiderman. Allard was frightened, one could tell by the solemn gleam in his eyes.

"Come on, Allard. We don't want the white folks to say that a gifted colored child was late, now do we?"

"Daddy, do I have to go? I don't want to go!"

Vida wasn't much help. She cleaned behind Jane, who was folding the lunch bags, muttering, "I don't understand this. I just don't understand this."

"Daddy, I am not colored. I am a Negro," Allard announced while clinging to the ceiling.

"That's my boy. That's exactly what you tell them, too." Greer chuckled.

Vida kept on, "I don't know why they have to go to the white folks' school. I just don't understand."

Greer patted Vida on her shoulders, sighing, "It's the law, Mama. Remember, I told you separate and equal was not separate and equal, just separate? Remember that?"

Jane looked at every one of her youngsters. Were they all ready? Did they look nice and clean and just like she wanted to remember them? She mustn't think like that. Nothing was going to happen.

"Mama, my shirt don't fit." Allard fidgeted.

"Your shirt doesn't fit," Jane said.

"No. It don't."

"No, it doesn't," Betsy chimed.

"That's what I *said*," Allard answered, indignant.

"Why does my child have to live round all these niggahs and talk so low?" Vida asked Jane in her most sincere voice.

"Mama, he's on his way right now to a white school." Jane was getting mad with everybody.

"But he talks like a niggah."

"Allard, you must be the niggah them white folks talk about. Grandma says you sound like one. Pickaninny.[2] Blackie. Boot."

"Charlie, you shut up. You're going to scare Allard to death." Jane was ready for them to go now.

"I was just practicing, Aunt Jane. I was preparing Allard for what's coming round the corner."

"All that's coming round the corner is the bus, Charlie. Stop filling the children's minds with mess."

"Aunt Jane, it's not mess. Look at all these colored children being an experiment. What do you think those white folks gonna say? We ain't nothing permanent. Niggahs come and go and die. Emmett Till[3] was my age, Aunt Jane."

"That's enough, Charlie. The Lord will see us through all this."

[2] a black child; used disparagingly

[3] a fifteen-year-old boy who was kidnapped and lynched in Mississippi in 1955

"But Aunt Jane, you think they're gonna pass us by, cause Betsey's gifted or Allard's so smart, or Sharon's only so dark? You think we can't be lynched? You think they don't see us for who we are? That's being fool—"

"Hush up that nonsense, you hoodlum northern trash," Vida interrupted.

"Mama, please don't say that. The children are agitated, that's all." Jane pulled her hands through her hair which was dampened with tears and sweat she'd been pushing up her forehead.

"Greer, let's go. Please, can we go?"

"The children don't seem so organized, Jane."

"Dammit, Greer, between you, the Supreme Court, the buses and the boys, I think I might die. I swear, I think I just might die."

Charlie leaned over to Allard, whispering, "We gonna get some white tail and say we did it for Emmett Till."

"Tail, I don't want any tail, Charlie."

"Hush your filthy mouth, you hear me? Hush!" Vida shouted.

Jane pulled Greer close to her. "Let's get out of here." As she went out the door, Jane turned and waved kisses back to her children. She wept on Greer's shoulder all the way to work.

Vida watched the children line up, military style, to go to their individual bus stops. She shook her head as the chant she heard them shouting reached into the quiet of the house.

All they can say is it's the law
All they can say is it's the law
Do they do it? Do they do it?
Naw.

Then Charlie's voice saying: "Does a peckerwood[4] hit you in the head during math?" Margot echoing, "Do the police watch you count your own money at the store?" Then Betsey adding, "Do white boys pull up your dress to see a niggah's behind?"

"No, not to see your behind. To see if you got a tail," Charlie answered. "It's the law and it's a mess. Hey, we gonna miss our buses," Charlie cried, alarmed.

"So what?" Betsey shouted for the whole neighborhood to hear: "We misst our buses. Who would give a damn? White folks wish our feet didn't even touch their holy ground. So what, we miss our buses? Who you think gonna come, Eisenhower, Faubus? Po' white trash with guns gonna escort us to our classes and make us eat the flag, while they tell us how slavery really wasn't quite so bad."

Off they went, belligerent, afraid and feeling totally put upon.

The brigade scattered at Union Boulevard.

"I get the number four."

"I'm catching the twelve."

"I'm heading southwest."

[4] a rural white Southerner; used disparagingly

"I don't wanta go," Allard pleaded.

"So what niggah? It's the law." That's all Charlie had to say. And they went their separate ways.

Vida wandered round the house picking up this and that: a ribbon, a crayon, a dustball. They got some nerve, those foolish urchins. They've got the honor of being Americans. They free and smart. They got good blood. And all they got on their minds is how it was in slavery times, as if we came from slaves. What a mess they've made of our genealogy, everybody knows we were freedmen. Then Vida stopped that train of thought, cause in order to be a freedman somebody would have had to be a slave and that concept did not compute.

When Betsey got to her new school, it loomed like a granite tomb over her head. Nobody spoke to her, so she didn't speak to them. It was like they were all dead. The white children weren't dirty or anything. They didn't even have red necks as far as she could tell, but they didn't smile at her the way she was usedta Susan Linda grinning at the corner of the schoolyard. This time Betsey had the whole corner to herself. Wherever she stepped, the other children found somewhere else to go. It was the first time Betsey knew she was someplace, yet felt no evidence of it. Maybe they couldn't see her. No, Betsey knew better than that. They chose not to, like the color of her skin was a blight. Betsey wisht it would rub off. She'd rub coloredness all over the damn place. Then where would they go to get away from the niggahs?

Mrs. Leon was the first person to address her by her name, Elizabeth Brown. In a linen suit and a tailored blouse with a blue bow at the collar, Mrs. Leon looked like a big little girl to Betsey. But at least Mrs. Leon didn't seem to think there was anything strange about her.

"Class, this is our new pupil, Betsey, I think she likes to be called. Is that right?"

"Yes, M'am."

"Well, you have a seat behind Jan there at the right, and we'll start our geography lessons. All your books should be in your desk. Let me know if you are missing anything." Mrs. Leon smiled.

Betsey thought maybe Mrs. Leon wasn't white at all, maybe she was passing, like in that book *Imitation of Life*. Or maybe she was what Jane called "well-meaning white people." At any rate Mrs. Leon broke the ice and the thrill of a new place and new faces came over Betsey as easily as the shadows had blackened her path.

It was luck or planning on Mrs. Leon's part, but the geography lesson had all to do with Africa. Greer had insisted that his children know every emerging African state's name and location, so Betsey was soaring with information. It turned out that the children didn't hate her actually, they just didn't know what to do with her. They'd never seen colored who didn't work for them or playing in some part of town nobody wanted to live in. But as the words Ghana, Nigeria, Sierra Leone, and Senegal rolled off Betsey's tongue, they sounded as romantic and elegant as

France, Germany, Alsace-Lorraine, or Bulgaria. Nobody could sing the words to "Rockin' Robin" at recess, but they played hop-scotch the same. One girl with wavy blond hair kept kosher, which Betsey didn't understand. She'd ask Jane. Another girl with brown hair and blue-green eyes, Randa, asked if Betsey would show her how to jump double-dutch. Betsey did her best, but the rhythm just wasn't coming from the rope-twirlers. Then the bell rang.

Betsey went back to Mrs. Leon with hopes things might get even better. The children who stayed away from her were as unswerving in their obstinance as Betsey was becoming optimistic about her new experience. Would she become one of them? Betsey often thought Susan Linda was most colored, cause she was too poor to be really white. There was the possibility of them rubbing off on her instead of her rubbing off on them. A fast trip to the girls' lavatory relieved Betsey of that dilemma. She'd go home just as brown as she'd arrived. Everybody at home would recognize her. No two ways about it. She was still Betsey Brown.

But the new school, Dewey School, would never be like her real school. It wasn't till the bus eased up Delmar Boulevard and the colored people were going on about their business, carrying things from the dry cleaners, going up the stairs to their apartments or the beauty shops, lingering by the corners exchanging tales, waiting in line for fried fish or shrimp, slinging barbeque sauce over ribs and burgers, playing honest-to-God double-dutch and liking it, that Betsey felt like she was at home. When she got off the streetcar Veejay and Eugene were waiting for her.

"Girl, we been here for three trolleys. How far is that place?"

"Oh Veejay, I'm so glad to see you." Betsey hugged her lost friend for dear life. It was so good to be around her own kind, friends who understood her already. Eugene was pleased nothing had happened to disturb his girl. Mr. Robinson served them all chocolate sundaes with cherries and teeny nuts all the way around.

"You made a step forward for the race today, Betsey. I'm real proud of you." Mr. Robinson knew most of Betsey's comings and goings. His pharmacy was right next to the trolley stop, so if you were going somewhere Mr. Robinson knew. He also knew if you didn't go somewhere. One time Betsey'd tried to make-believe she got on the trolley to go to her piano lesson, but she just stood at the door and then jumped off. She stayed the whole time in the store with Mr. Robinson and then tried to walk home as if she'd been to her lesson with that fat old Mr. Benjamin who had nine children and a wife who sang opera. But Mr. Robinson had already called her parents to say she was staying in the pharmacy an awfully long time.

Jane let Betsey go on about the Benjamin children and their West Indian accents, how well she was doing with her scales and the new Chopin piece, when Greer mentioned casually that Mr. Robinson had said what good company she'd been all afternoon, business was kind of slow, Betsey was a wonderful child to talk to. What a licking that led to. So Betsey never tried to do anything in front of Mr. Robinson anymore. He stuck with the grown-ups, but today he was proud of her. Maybe he'd call Jane and Greer and tell them that, too.

Eugene walked Betsey home after they'd walked Veejay round to Charlotte Ann's where she was visiting till her mother got off work.

"I can't wait for you every day, Betsey. I've got practice, but I was worried today. What with all them white people. Never know what they'll do."

"They weren't nearly as bad as I thought they'd be, Eugene. Honest. Why I even made one friend, Randa. But they're not like us. That's the truth. They can't dance or play rope. They don't talk the same. It's almost like going to another country."

"Well, you be sure and tell me if one of those white boys messes with you, you hear?"

"Uh huh. I'll tell you." Betsey wanted to throw her arms round Eugene's neck and kiss him a Roscoe and Regina kiss for saying what he'd just said. He was willing to protect her. He wanted to know if anything happened to her. She held herself back, smiling from one braid to the other.

"Eugene, I'm really glad you like me that much."

Eugene blushed a bit and was on his way. Betsey didn't know from day to day when she'd see him, but she knew he was there if she needed him.

The children's commutes put the dinner back by an

hour and a half. Jane and Greer were home before everybody except Allard, who kept exclaiming: "Mama, they didn't kill me. Look, Mama, I'm alive."

"Yes, you are, Allard. You are very much alive. I told you not all the white people were evil. There's evil in every group."

"Yeah, Charlie's evil."

"No, Charlie isn't evil. He's having growing pains, that's all."

"Look, Daddy, I'm alive. The white folks didn't kill me."

Margot and Sharon luckily had each other for support at their school, where nothing in particular happened. They were just dirty and fuzzy-headed enough to let Jane know they'd spent their time playing and were out of danger. The missing Charlie changed the scene entirely, when he walked in with a torn shirt and a black eye. Everybody ran up to him. Vida went to get a piece of cold beef to put over that eye. Jane hugged him as she loosened the remnants of the pressed shirt from her nephew's back.

"Those dirty guineas callt me a niggah, Uncle Greer. They callt me a niggah. I didn't have any choice. I had to defend myself."

"All you could think to do is use your hands, Charles. Is that all you've learned? Fighting white folks won't change their minds. It just makes them meaner. Now you sit down and let's take a look at what's happened to you. How many were there, Charlie?" Greer asked, quite serious.

"Five greasy-headed wop bastards."

"Charlie, you didn't learn that language here, and I won't have it in my house." Jane was exasperated. Of all the children she'd been worried about, Charlie was the last one she thought would have trouble. It was his temper. No. That was a lie. It was the white people. No. It was Greer filling the children's heads with stories of heroes and standing up for yourself at any cost. Jane didn't know what to do but soothe the aching bones of her sister's son and listen.

"Why didn't you get the principal or the school guard, Charles?" Greer went on.

"What for? So they could all gang up on me? I'm not going back there."

"Yes you are. What's the point of having stood up for yourself if you're going to back down your next move."

Greer was thinking maybe he should have taken each of the children to school himself. That way everybody would know that there was somebody to be reckoned with if so much as a hair on the head of a Brown was put out of place. Jane didn't quite know how to handle this. She'd promised Catholic schools at the first sign of trouble, but she and Greer also had a pact, which was not to contradict each other in front of the children.

"But Uncle Greer, there's more of them than there are of me. I'm gonna carry me some of my fellas back over there. Let them see what a pack of 'niggahs' can do to their greasy-just-off-the-boat asses."

"Charles, I did say that was quite enough of that language. The other children don't need to hear you talking like that. It won't help anything."

"Look, Charlie, the guineas didn't kill me either," Allard jumped in.

"See what I mean, Charles, you've got to be careful what you say."

When Vida returned with the meat for Charlie's eye, she chirped: "See, there's no sense going where you're not wanted. White folks are enough trouble far off, no need to be all up under them too." With that Vida set the little steak on Charlie's face and examined the bruises on his chest.

"Looks just like when they pulled my great-uncle Julius out his house to lynch him. That's what it looks like." Vida just shook her head.

Jane looked up, startled. "Mama, you weren't even alive when that happened."

"There's some things you never forget, Jane. It runs in you blood memory. That's what it does."

"Oh, Mama."

"Charlie, tomorrow you and I will be going to that school together. We'll see who wants to take on the Golden Gloves Champion of 1941 and the latest hero of the race."

"Really, Uncle Greer? You'll go there with me? I don't want it to look like you're seeing to a little guy like Allard or nothing."

"No, we'll go, two men together."

"Y'all best leave those white folks alone." Vida slipped away to the yard where there were only green things. They understood her ways of thinking. Grow in your own patch. Stay put and blossom.

Jane suddenly realized there was no dinner ready. She left the family staring at Charlie, while Greer tried to make the best of it, boosting the spirits of the new pioneers with the family chant, "The work of the Negro is never done."

Yet Charlie's bruises brought home what they'd all been worried about. The vengeance of the white people. It could have been any one of them, Mrs. Leon or no Mrs. Leon. Were there enough "well-meaning white folks" to outdo the ordinary ones who'd attack a boy like Charlie five to one?

Betsey counted her blessings. She looked at her sisters and Allard, grateful no harm had befallen them. She thought not being spoken to was the kindness of the Lord compared to what Charlie'd faced. But now there was the issue of safety. Daddy couldn't be everywhere with everyone every day. Somebody had to earn a living. It was clear to Betsey the police weren't earning theirs.

"Girls, come help me with the supper," Jane shouted from the kitchen.

"All right, Mama," but none of them moved. They were waiting for some sign from Charlie that everything was all right again.

"You heard Aunt Jane, go get dinner ready, would you? I'm hungry."

Charlie could talk fine, but his words were slurred cause he wanted to cry too. He couldn't bear the burden of the whole race all by himself. Not every day. Alone. He was so glad Uncle Greer had decided to go with him just once. He'd let those guineas, oh, those people, know he wasn't alone in this. Not by a long shot.

Vida'd come in from her garden and run everybody, including Jane, out of the kitchen. She said there was too much mess going on in the house, and cooking gave her peace of mind. The children needed to do their lessons, so the white folks would know they weren't any dummies.

"Look, Grandma, the white folks didn't kill me."

"Of course not, Allard. They only kill little boys who don't mind."

"Mama! That was an inappropriate answer," Jane said, irritated.

"Well, I told him what I think."

"Allard, the white people aren't going to kill anybody. What happened to Charlie happens everywhere, even between Negroes themselves. Remember what I told you: there's evil folks in every walk of life. Their color has nothing to do with it."

"That's not what Charlie said. He said there was five of them and one of him."

"Allard, Charlie's mad right now. Everything he says when he's mad isn't true."

"No, I saw it. He's got a black eye."

"Mama, you know those white boys beat on Charlie," Sharon added adamantly.

"See what I told you bout messing with them white folks." Vida was sprinkling the greens with cayenne, thinking maybe she ought to give each of the children a little bit to throw on the whites who bothered them.

"Mama, this is not the time to discourage them."

"I'm not discouraging them. I'm encouraging them to mind their ways round those people."

"They are not 'those people,' they are just some other people. Mama, please, let's not argue."

"Well, if they bother me, I'm gonna set em on fire, that's what I'm gointa do," Allard declared.

"You'll do no such thing."

"Yes I will. They go up in flames to glory. Won't they, Grandma?"

"I'm not sure that's where they'll go, Allard."

"Mama, how could you say such a thing when you know Allard has a predilection for fire-setting. I just can't believe it."

"Well, why don't you take a look at Charlie's eye and see what's to be believed, then?"

"Greer, Greer, take me out of here. I have to go somewhere and clear my head. Tween the white folks, Mama, the Supreme Court, the buses, the boys, the girls at that stage, oh my God, Greer, please get me out of here."

Greer stood in the doorway of the kitchen toward the back steps.

"Come on upstairs, Jane. It's quiet. I'm going to take all the children to school tomorrow, make no mistake. Right now, though, I think I better take care of you."

"I just don't know how much of this I can take," Jane murmured as she and Greer slowly walked to their room.

"It's not that bad, is it?" Greer stopped at the bend in the stairs where the children couldn't spy on them and wrapped his arms around her.

"It's not my idea of a quiet family life."

"These aren't peaceful times, Jane." Greer kissed her temple and held her face in his hand. "You're as strong as I am. We'll make it through this and we'll reminisce bout the evening you were storming about, saying you were losing your mind. The evening I asked for a little bit of loving at quarter of six."

"Now?"

"Yep."

"What about dinner and the children?"

"They'll be right there, believe me, they aren't going anywhere."

"Must be you think I'm crazy, too. All you can think I have to do is to go off making love to you at quarter of six in the evening. I couldn't have conceived this is where we'd be thirteen years from then. And thirteen years from now?"

"We'll still be together, sweetheart. How about a tango, a bolero, a samba, a mambo?"

Jane snuggled up to Greer. "Just nothing too African, you hear. The bed can't take it."

Betsey peeked around the corner of the landing they were on before they ran off and locked their door.

"There's never enough when you're really in love, is there Mommy . . ."

A Brief Moment in the Life of Angus Bethune

Chris Crutcher

Sometimes, when I stand back and take a good look, I think my parents are ambassadors from hell. Two of them, at least, the biological ones, the big ones.

Four parents are what I have altogether, not unlike a whole lot of other kids. But quite unlike a whole lot of other kids, there ain't a hetero among 'em. My dad's divorced and remarried, and my mom's divorced and remarried, so my mathematical account of my family suggests simply another confused teenager from a broken home. But my dads aren't married to my moms. They're married to *each other*. Same with my moms.

However, that's not the principal reason I sometimes see my so-called real parents as emissaries from way down under. As a matter of fact, that frightening little off-season trade took place prior to—though not *much* prior to—my birth, so until I began collecting expert feedback from friends at school, somewhere along about fourth grade, I perceived my situation as relatively normal.

No, what really hacks me off is that they didn't conceive me in some high tech fashion that would have allowed them to dip into an alternative gene pool for my physical goodies. See, when people the size of my parents decide to reproduce, they usually dig a pit and crawl down in there together for several days. Really, I'm surprised someone in this family doesn't have a trunk. Or a blowhole. I swear my gestation period was three years and seven months.

You don't survive a genetic history like that unscathed. While farsighted parents of other infants my age were pre-enrolling their kids four years ahead into elite preschools, my dad was hounding the World Wrestling Federation to hold a spot for me sometime in the early 1990s. I mean, my mom had to go to the husky section of Safeway to buy me Pampers.

I'm a big kid.

And they named me Angus. God, a name like Angus Bethune would tumble *Robert Redford* from a nine and a half to a four, and I ain't no Robert Redford.

"Angus is a cow," I complained to my stepmother, Bella, the day in first grade I came home from school early for punching the bearer of that sad information in the stomach.

"Your mother must have had a good reason for naming you that," she said.

"For naming me after a cow?"

"You can't go around punching everyone who says that to you," she warned.

"Yes, I can," I said.

"Angus is a cow," I said to my mother when she got home from her job at Westhead Trucking firm. "You guys named me after a cow."

"Your father's uncle was named Angus," she said, stripping off her outer shirt with a loud sigh, then plopping into her easy chair with a beer, wearing nothing but her bra, a bra, I might add, that could well have floated an ejected fighter pilot to safety.

"So my father's uncle was named after a cow, too," I said. "What did *he* think of that?"

"Actually," Mom said, "I think he was kind of proud. Angus was quite a farmer, you know."

"Jesus help me," I said, and went to my room.

As Angus, the fat kid with perverted parents, I've had my share of adjustment problems, though it isn't as bad as it sounds. My parents' gene pool wasn't a *total* sump. Dad's family had all kinds of high-school shot put record holders and hammer throwers and even a gridiron hero or two, and my mom's sister almost made it to the Olympic trials in speed skating, so I was handed a fair-size cache of athletic ability. I am *incredibly* quick for a fat kid, and I have world-class reflexes. It is nearly impossible for the defensive lineman across from me to shake me, such are my anticipatory skills, and when I'm on defense, I need only to lock in on a running back's hips to zero in on the tackle. I cannot be shaken free. Plus you don't have to dig *too* deep in our ancestral remains to find an IQ safely into three digits, so grades come pretty easy to me. But I'd sure be willing to go into the winter trade meetings and swap reflexes, biceps, and brain cells, lock, stock, and barrel, for a little physical beauty.

Which brings me to tonight. I don't want you to think I spend *all* my life bitching about being shortchanged in the Tom Cruise department or about having parents a shade to the left of middle on your normal bell-shaped sexual curve; but tonight is a big night, and I don't want the blubbery bogeymen or the phantoms of sexual perversity, who usually pop up to point me out for public mockery, mucking it up for me. I want *normal.* I want *socially acceptable.* See, I was elected Senior Winter Ball King, which means for about one minute I'll be featured gliding across the floor beneath the crimson and gold crepe paper streamers at Lake Michigan High School with Melissa Lefevre, the girl of my dreams—and only my dreams—who was elected Senior Winter Ball Queen. For that minute we'll be out there alone.

Alone with Melissa Lefevre.

Now I don't want to go into the tomfoolery that must have gone on behind the scenes to get me elected to such a highly regarded post because to tell you the truth, I can't even imagine. I mean, it's a joke, I know that. I just don't know whose. It's a hell of a good one, though, because someone had to coax a plurality of more than five hundred seniors to forgo casting their ballots for any of a number of bona fide Adonises to write in the name of a cow. At first I tried to turn it down, but Granddad let me know right quick I'd draw a lot more attention if I made a fuss than if I acted as if I were the logical choice—indeed, the only choice—and went right along. Granddad is the man who taught me to be a dignified fat kid. "Always remember these words, and live by 'em," he said after my third suspension from kindergarten for fighting. "*Screw 'em.* Anybody doesn't like the way you look, screw 'em."

And that's just what I've done, because my grandfather—on my dad's side—is one righteous dude, and as smart as they come in an extra-large wide-body sport coat. Sometimes I've screwed 'em by punching them in the nose, and sometimes by walking away. And sometimes by joining them—you know, laughing at myself. That's the one that works best. But when my temper is quick, it likes to speak first, and often as not someone's lying on the floor in a pool of nose fluids before I remember what a hoot it is to have the names of my mother and father dragged through the mud or my body compared with the Michelin tire man.

So you see, slowly but surely I'm getting all this under control. I don't mind that my detractors—who are legion—will wonder aloud tonight whether it is Melissa or I who is the Winter Ball Queen, a playful reference to my folks' quirky preferences, and I don't mind that I'll likely hear, "Why do they just swim up on the beach like that?" at least three times. What I mind is that during those few seconds when Melissa and I have the floor to ourselves, all those kids, friend and foe, will be watching me *dance*. Now, I've chronicled the majority of my maladies here, but none remotely approaches my altogether bankrupt sense of rhythm. When it comes to clapping his hands or stomping his feet, Angus Bethune is completely, absolutely, and, most of all, irreversibly brain dead.

I've known about the dance for three weeks now. I even know the name of the song, though I don't recognize it, and I went out and spent hard-earned money on dance lessons, dance lessons that sent not one but two petite, anorexic-looking rookie Arthur Murray girls off sharpening their typing skills to apply to Kelly Services. Those girls had some sore pods.

I've been planning for Melissa Lefevre for a long time. I fell in love with her in kindergarten, when she dared a kid named Alex Immergluck to stick his tongue on a car bumper in minus-thirty-five-degree weather for calling her a "big, fat, snot-nosed deadbeat," a term I'm sure now that was diagnostic of his homelife, but that at the time served only to call up Melissa's anger. Being a fat kid, I was interested in all the creative retaliatory methods I could get to store in the computer for later use, and when I saw the patch of Alex's tongue stuck tight to the bumper as he screamed down the street, holding his bleeding mouth, I knew I was in the company of genius. And such lovely genius it was. God, from kindergarten on, Melissa was that tan, sinewy-legged blond girl with the brown eyes that just make you ache. You ache a lot more when you're a fat kid, though, because you know she was put on the earth, out of your reach, only to make you feel bad. You have no business trying to touch her.

But at that same time my grandfather—a huge silver-haired Rolls-Royce of a grandfather—kept telling me over and over I could have any damn thing I wanted. He told me that down under that sleeping bag of globules I wore beneath my skin beat the heart of a lion and the body of Jack La Lanne. In fact, in the fifth grade Granddad took me down to San Francisco on Jack's sixty-fifth birthday to let me watch him swim to Alcatraz with his hands cuffed behind him, towing a boat on a line with his teeth. He did it, he really did. He still does.

Granddad also took me to San Francisco to see some gay people; but we went to a place called Polk Street, and it didn't help much. I mean, my parents are working folks who are with only the person they're with, and Polk Street was filled with people looking like they were headed for a Tandy leather swap meet. Maybe it helped, though. At least my parents looked more normal to me, although my mother could pass for Bruiser of the Week about fifty-two times in any given year, so *normal* is a relative term.

The bottom line, though, no matter how my grandfather tried to convince me otherwise, was that Melissa Lefevre would remain a Fig Newton of my imagination throughout my school years, and no matter how hard Granddad primed me, I would never have the opportunity for any conversation with Melissa other than the one in my head. Until tonight. Tonight I'll *have* to talk to her. If I don't, she'll have only my dancing by which to remember me, which is like Mrs. Fudd remembering Elmer for his hair. It'd be a damn shame.

All I really want is my moment with her. I have no illusions, no thoughts of her being struck blind and asking me to take her home. When you're different, on the down side, you learn to live from one scarce rich moment to the next, no matter the distance in between. You become like a camel in a vast scorched desert dotted with precious few oases, storing those cool, watery moments in your hump, assuring survival until you stumble upon the next.

All I want is my moment.

So here I sit, my rented burgundy tux lying across my bed like a dropcloth waiting to be unfolded on the floor of the Sistine Chapel, digging deep into my reserves for the courage not to crumble, hoping for the power to call up the vision of the decent guy I know I am rather than the short-fused, round clown-jock so many people see. What can

Melissa be thinking? She'll be there with someone else, of course, so her winter Nightmare on Elm Street will last but a few minutes at most. She's probably telling herself as I sit here that it's like a trip to the dentist. No matter how badly he's going to hurt you, no matter how many bare nerves he drills or how many syringes of Novocain he explodes into the roof of your mouth, in an hour you'll walk out of there. And you'll still be alive.

Of course, Melissa hasn't seen me dance.

My dad was in an hour ago, looking sadly at me sitting here on the side of my bed in my underwear next to this glorious tuxedo, which, once on, will undoubtedly cast me as a giant plum. Dad's the one who escorted me to Roland's Big and Tall to have me fitted, and to make sure I got something that would be comfortable. He's a sensitive guy, one who has always scouted uncharted waters for me in an attempt to clear away at least the huge logs, to render those waters a little more navigable.

He wore his Kissbusters T-shirt, with the universal stop sign—a circle with a slash through it—over huge red lips. I gave one to each of my four parents back in junior high when I negotiated the No Kissing Contract. ("I don't care who's with who or what you do in the sack at night," I screamed out of exasperation during one of our bimonthly "absence of malice get-togethers," designed by my parents to cement our extended family solidarity. "Just don't *kiss* in front of me! I'm in junior high now! Look! Under here!"

I said, raising my arms, pointing to the budding tufts of hair. "I got a bouquet of flowering pubiscus under each arm! And the jury's in: I like girls! The only people I want to see kissing are boys and girls! Not boys kissing boys. Not girls kissing girls! I want to see boys kissing girls! Understand? Hairy lips on smooth lips! Read mine! Boys . . . kissing . . . girls!" I started to walk out of the room, then whirled. "You know what I need? You ask me that all the time! 'Angus, are you suffering emotional harm because we're different? Angus, are you feeling angst? Angus, do you need help adjusting? Angus, do you want to see a therapist?' I'm not having trouble adjusting! I don't even know what angst is! I don't want to see a therapist! I just don't want to see you *kissing*! You want to know what I need? I'll tell you! Role models! Someone to show me how things are done! Don't you guys ever watch Oprah? Or Donahue?") It was a marvelous tantrum, and effective in that it resulted in the now-famous ironclad No Kissing Contract, which I have since, for my part, dissolved but to which they adhere as if it were the *Kama Sutra* itself. You will not here the smacking, sucking reverberations of lips parting in passion from lips in either of *my* happy homes.

"The cummerbund is good," Dad says. "It changes your lines, acts almost as a girdle. Don't keep the jacket buttoned for long, unbutton it early in the name of being casual. That way it won't pull tight where you bulge." Dad is the person most responsible for teaching men to dress a body ignored by the sensibilities of the world's clothiers. It was he who taught me to buy pants with a high waist and to go ahead through the embarrassment of giving the salesman my full waist size—instead of cheating a few inches to save face—so I could always get *all* of myself into my pants and leave nothing hanging over. He also drilled into me that it is a mortal sin for a fat man to buy a shirt that tucks in. In short, my father is most responsible for teaching me to dress like a big top.

As he stands staring at the tuxedo, his brain grinding out camouflage intelligence, I read his mind.

"Don't worry, Dad," I say. "I can handle this."

"You've had this girl on your mind a long time," he says sadly. "I don't want you to be hurt."

I say, "I'm not going to be hurt, Dad," thinking: Please don't make me take care of you, too.

Alexander, my stepdad, walks through the bedroom door, places a hand on Dad's shoulder, and guides him out of the room. He reappears in seconds. "Your father's a pain in the butt sometimes, huh," he says, "worrying about things you wouldn't even think about."

I say, "Yeah, he is. Only this time *I'm* thinking of them. How am I going to get through this night without looking like Moby Melon with a stick in my butt?"

Alexander nods and looks at my near-naked carcass. He is like an arrow, sleek and angular, the antithesis of my father. It is as if minor gods were given exactly enough clay to make two human forms but divided it up in a remedial math class. Alexander is also sensible—though somewhat obscure—where my father is romantic. "Superman's not brave," he says.

I look up. "What?"

"Superman. He's not brave."

"I'll send him a card."

Alexander smiles. "You don't understand. Superman's not brave. He's smart. He's handsome. He's even decent. But he's not brave."

I look at the tux, spread beside me, waiting. "Alexander, have I ever said it's hard to follow you sometimes?"

"He's indestructible," Alexander says. "You can't be brave when you're indestructible. It's guys like you and me that are brave, Angus. Guys who are different and can be crushed—and know it—but go out there anyway."

I looked at the tux. "I guess he wouldn't wear such an outrageous suit if he knew he looked like a blue and red Oldsmobile in it, would he?"

Alexander put his hand on my shoulder. "The tux looks fine, Angus." He left.

So now I stand at the door to the gym. The temperature is near zero, but I wear no coat because once inside, I want to stay cool as long as possible, to reduce the risk of the dike-bursting perspiration that has become my trademark. No pun intended. Melissa—along with almost everyone, I would guess—is inside, waiting to be crowned Queen of the Winter Ball before suffering the humiliation of being jerked across the dance floor by an escort who should have "GOODYEAR" tattooed the length of both sides. My fear is nearly paralyzing, to tell the truth, but I've faced down this monster before—though, admittedly, he gets more fierce every time—and I'll face him down again. When he beats me, I'm done.

Heads turn as I move through the door. I simulate drying my butt with a towel, hoping for a casual twist-and-shout move. Your king is here. Rejoice. Marsha Stanwick stands behind the ticket table, and I casually hand her mine, eyes straight ahead on the band, walking lightly on the balls of my feet, like Raymond Burr through a field of dog poop sundaes. I pause to let my eyes adjust, hoping to God an empty table will appear, allowing me to drop out of the collective line of sight. Miraculously one does, and I squat, eyes still glued to the band, looking for all the world like the rock and roll critic from the *Trib*. If my fans are watching, they're seeing a man who *cares* about music. I lightly tap my fingers to what I perceive to be the beat, blowing my cover to smithereens. I see Melissa on the dance floor with her boyfriend—a real jerk in my book, Rick Sanford—and my heart bursts against the walls of my chest, like in *Alien*. I order it back. A sophomore server leaves a glass of punch on the table, and I sip it slowly through the next song, after which the lead singer announces that the "royal couple" and their court are due behind the stage curtain in five minutes.

Tributaries of perspiration join at my rib cage to form

a raging torrent of sweat running toward my shoes as I silently hyperventilate, listening for my grandfather's voice, telling me to screw 'em, telling me once again I can do anything I want. I want my moment.

I rise to the head of the stage and look to see Melissa on her boyfriend's arm, coming toward me through the crowd parting on the dance floor. Sanford wears that cocky look, the one I remember from football, the one he wore continually until the day I wiped it off his face on the sideline during our first full-pad scrimmage. Golden Rick Sanford—Rick Running Back—danced his famous jig around end and turned upfield, thought he could juke me with a couple of cheap high school hip fakes, not realizing that *this* blimp was equipped with tracking radar. It took him almost fifteen seconds to get his wind back. Hacked him off big time, me being so fat and ugly. But now the look is back; we're in his element. He's country club; I'm country, a part of his crowd on the field only.

As they approach, I panic. The king has no clothes. I want to run. What am I doing here? What was I thinking of? Suddenly I'd give up my moment in a heartbeat for the right to disappear. What a fool, even to think . . .

They stand before me. "Angus, my man," Rick slurs, and I realize it's not a change of underwear he's carrying in that paper bag. "I'm turning this lovely thing over to you for a while. Give her a chance to make a comparison. You know, be a bit more humble."

Melissa drops her arm and smiles. She says, "Hi. Don't

pay any attention to him. He's drunk. And even without that, he's rude."

I smile and nod, any words far, far from my throat.

Melissa says, "Why don't we go on up?" and she takes my arm, leaving Rick's to hang limply at his side.

"Yeah," he says, squinting down at the paper sack in his hand, "why don't you go on up? You go right on up behind that curtain with my girl, snowball king."

Melissa drops my arm and grips his elbow. "Shut up," she whispers between her clenched teeth. "I'm warning you, Rick. Shut up."

Rick tears his arm away. "Enjoy yourself," he says to me, ignoring her. "Your campaign cost me a lot of money, probably close to two bucks a pound." He looks me up and down as couples at the nearest tables turn to stare. The heat of humiliation floods up through my collar, and I fear the worst will follow. I fear I'll cry. If I do, Rick's in danger because it's a law that rage follows my tears as surely as baby chicks trail after their mama. "Don't you be puttin' your puffy meat hooks on my girl," he says, and starts to poke me in the chest; but I look at his finger, and he thinks better.

Melissa takes my arm again and says, "Let's go."

We move two steps toward the stage, and Rick says, loud, "Got your rubber gloves, honey?"

I turn, feeling Melissa's urgent tug, pulling me toward the stage.

"What do you mean by that?" I ask quietly, knowing full well what he means by that.

"I wasn't talking to you, bigfoot," Rick says, looking past me to his girl. "I'm asking if my sweetie's got her rubber gloves."

Melissa says, "I hate you, Rick. I really do."

Rick ignores her. "Bigfoot comes from a high-risk home," he says. "Best wear your rubber gloves, honey, in case he has a cut."

In that instant I sweep his feet with mine, and he lands hard on the floor. He moves to get up, but I'm over him, crowding. When he tries to push himself up, I kick his hands out, following his next movements like a cow dog, mirroring him perfectly, trapping him there on the floor. No chaperon is in view, so it isn't totally out of hand yet. When he sees he can't rise, I kneel, sweat pouring off my forehead like rain. Softly, very softly, I say, "You may not like how my parents live. But they've been together since 1971—monogamous as the day is long. That's a low-risk group, Rick. The only person at high risk right now is you."

He looks into my eyes and he knows I mean it, knows I'm past caring about my embarrassment. "Okay, man," he says, raising his hands in surrender, "just having a little fun."

I'm apologizing to Melissa all the way up the backstage stairs, but she's not having any. "You should have stomped on his throat," she says, and I involuntarily visualize Alex Immergluck clutching at his bleeding mouth in the freezing cold next to the car bumper. "If you get another chance, I'll pay you money."

At the side door to the stage I say, "Speaking of embarrassment, there's something you need to know."

She waits.

"I can't dance."

Melissa smiles. "Not everyone's Nureyev," she says. "We'll survive."

I say, "Yeah, well, not everyone's Quasimodo either. I didn't say I can't dance *well.* I said I can't dance. Good people have been badly hurt trying to dance with me."

We're near the risers on the stage now, and our "court," made up of juniors and sophomores, stands below the spot at the top where we are to be crowned. Melissa hushes me as we receive instructions from the senior class adviser. There will be trumpeting, the crowning by last year's royalty, followed by a slow march down the portable steps to the gym floor to begin the royal dance.

We take our places. The darkness of the stage and the wait are excruciating. "What did he mean, my campaign cost him a lot of money?" I whisper.

"Never mind."

I snort a laugh and say, "I can take it."

"He's rich, and he's rude," she says. "I'm embarrassed I'm with him." She pauses, and slides her arm in mine. "I'm not with him. It was supposed to be a lesson for me. . . ."

The curtains part as the trumpets blare.

I gaze out into the spotlights, smiling like a giant "Have a Nice Day" grape. The introduction of last year's king and queen begins, and they move toward us from stage left and right to relinquish their crowns to us. It all would be unbelievably ridiculous even if they weren't crowning King Angus the Fat. Without moving her lips, Melissa says, "I picked a slow song. We don't have to move much. Dance close to me. When you feel me lean, you lean. Whatever you do, don't listen to the music. It'll just mess you up. Trust me. My brother's like you. Just follow."

She grips my arm as the royal march starts and leads me down the risers to the portable steps leading to the dance floor. I have surrendered. If I am to survive this, it will be through the will of Melissa Lefevre.

Somehow I remember to hand her the traditional single long-stemmed red rose, and she takes it in her hand, smiling, then pulls me tight. She says, "Shadow me."

A part of me stays to concentrate, but another part goes to heaven. In my wildest dreams I could never have imagined Melissa Lefevre being *nice* to me in my moment, would never have *dared* imagine holding her tight without feeling pushy and ugly and *way* out of line. She whispers, "Relax," into my ear, and I mechanically follow through a song I'd never heard, not that it would make a difference. When I'm finally relaxed enough and know I'm going to live, the words to "Limelight" filter into my head, and I realize I'm *in* it. Like the songwriter, I fear it yet am drawn to it like a shark to a dangling toe.

"Alan Parsons," she whispers in my ear. "Good lyrics.

I love 'em. And I hate 'em. That's what makes a song *good*."

I wouldn't know a good song from a hot rock; I'm just hoping it's a *long* song. Feeling greedy now, I want my moment to last.

"Angus?"

"Yeah?"

"Do you ever get tired of who you are?"

I pull back a second, but it's like Lois Lane releasing Superman's hand twenty thousand feet in the air. She falls. I pull close again. "Do you know who you're talking to?"

I feel her smile. "Yeah," she says, "I thought so. I know it's not the same, but it's not always so great looking the way I do, either. I pay, too."

She's right. I think it's not the same.

"Want to know something about me?" she asks, and I think: I'd like to know *anything* about you.

I say, "Sure."

"I'm bulimic. Do you know what that is?"

I smile. "I'm a fat kid with faggot parents who's been in therapy on and off for eighteen years," I say. "Yes, I know what that is. It means when you eat too much, you chuck it up so you don't turn out to look like me."

"Close enough for discussion purposes. Don't worry, I'm in therapy for it," she says, noticing my concern. "A *lot* of pretty girls are."

"Actually," I say, "I even tried it once, but when I stuck

my finger down my throat, I was still hungry and I almost ate my arm."

Melissa laughs and holds me tighter. "You're the only person I've told except for the people in my therapy group; I just wanted you to know things aren't always as they appear. Would you do me a favor?"

"If it doesn't involve more than giving up my life," I say, feeling wonderful because Melissa isn't a goddess anymore and because that doesn't change the way I feel about her.

"Would you leave with me?"

My foot clomps onto her delicate toe.

"Concentrate," she says. Then: "Would you?"

"You mean leave this dance? Leave this dance with you?"

I feel her nod.

I consider. "At least I don't turn into a pumpkin at midnight. I'm a pumpkin already."

"I like how you stood up for your family. It must be hard. Defending them all the time, I mean."

"Compared to me, a boy named Sue had it made," I say.

The music ends; all dancers stop and clap politely. "I want to dance one more," Melissa says. "A fast one."

"I'll wait over by the table."

"No. I want to dance it with you."

"You don't understand," I say. "When I dance to the beat of rock and roll, decent folks across this great land quake in their boots."

She holds my hand tightly. "Listen. Do what you did

when you wouldn't let Rick up. Don't listen to the music; just follow me the way you followed him."

I try to protest; but the band breaks into "Bad Moon Rising," and the dance floor erupts. Melissa pushes me back gently, and out of panic, I zero in, locking on her hips as I would a running back's. I back away as she comes at me, mirroring her every move, top to bottom. She cuts to the sideline, and I meet her, dancing upfield nose to nose. As the band heats up, I remain locked in; though her steps become more and more intricate, she cannot shake me. A crowd gathers, and I'm trapped inside a cheering circle, actually performing the unheard of: I'm Angus Bethune, Fat Man Extraordinaire, dancing in the limelight with Melissa Lefevre, stepping outside the oppressive prison of my body to fly to the beat of Creedence Clearwater Revival.

When the drummer bangs the last beat, the circle erupts in celebration, and I take a long, low bow. Melissa is clapping wildly. She reaches across and wipes a drop of sweat from my brow with her finger. When she touches the finger to her tongue, I tell God he can take me now.

"You bitch!" Rick yells at the door as I help Melissa into her coat. "You bitch! You practiced with this tub of lard! You guys been getting together dancing. You bitch. You set me up." He turns to me. "I oughta take you out, fat boy," he says, but his unimaginative description can't touch my glory.

I put up a finger and wag it side to side in front of his

nose. "You know the difference between you and me, Sanford?"

He says, "There's a *lot* of differences between us, lardo. You couldn't count the differences between us."

"That's probably true," I say, closing my fist under his nose. "But the one that matters right now is that I can make *you* ugly."

He stares silently at my fist.

I say, "Don't even think about it. Next to dancing, that's my strong suit."

X: A Fabulous Child's Story

Lois Gould

Once upon a time, a baby named X was born. This baby was named X so that nobody could tell whether it was a boy or a girl. Its parents could tell, of course, but they couldn't tell anybody else. They couldn't even tell Baby X, at first.

You see, it was all part of a very important Secret Scientific Xperiment, known officially as Project Baby X. The smartest scientists had set up this Xperiment at a cost of Xactly 23 billion dollars and 72 cents, which might seem like a lot for just one baby, even a very important Xperimental baby. But when you remember the prices of things like strained carrots and stuffed bunnies, and popcorn for the movies and booster shots for camp, let alone

28 shiny quarters from the tooth fairy, you begin to see how it adds up.

Also, long before Baby X was born, all those scientists had to be paid to work out the details of the Xperiment, and to write the *Official Instruction Manual* for Baby X's parents and, most important of all, to find the right set of parents to bring up Baby X. These parents had to be selected very carefully. Thousands of volunteers had to take thousands of tests and answer thousands of tricky questions. Almost everybody failed because, it turned out, almost everybody really wanted either a baby boy or a baby girl, and not Baby X at all. Also, almost everybody was afraid that a Baby X would be a lot more trouble than a boy or girl. (They were probably right, the scientists admitted, but Baby X needed parents who wouldn't *mind* the Xtra trouble.)

There were families with grandparents named Milton and Agatha, who didn't see why the baby couldn't be named Milton or Agatha instead of X, even if it *was* an X. There were families with aunts who insisted on knitting tiny dresses and uncles who insisted on sending tiny baseball mitts. Worst of all, there were families that already had other children who couldn't be trusted to keep the secret. Certainly not if they knew the secret was worth 23 billion dollars and 72 cents-and all you had to do was take one little peek at Baby X in the bathtub to know if it was a boy or a girl.

But, finally, the scientists found the Joneses, who really

wanted to raise an X more than any other kind of baby—no matter how much trouble it would be. Ms. and Mr. Jones had to promise they would take equal turns caring for X, and feeding it, and singing it lullabies. And they had to promise never to hire any baby-sitters. The government scientists knew perfectly well that a baby-sitter would probably peek at X in the bathtub, too.

The day the Joneses brought their baby home, lots of friends and relatives came over to see it. None of them knew about the secret Xperiment, though. So the first thing they asked was what kind of a baby X was. When the Joneses smiled and said, "It's an X!" nobody knew what to say. They couldn't say, "Look at her cute little dimples!" And they couldn't say, "Look at his husky little biceps!" And they couldn't even say just plain "kitchy-coo." In fact, they all thought the Joneses were playing some kind of rude joke.

But, of course, the Joneses were not joking. "It's an X" was absolutely all they would say. And that made the friends and relatives very angry. The relatives all felt embarrassed about having an X in the family. "People will think there's something wrong with it!" some of them whispered. "There *is* something wrong with it!" others whispered back.

"Nonsense!" the Joneses told them all cheerfully. "What could possibly be wrong with this perfectly adorable X?"

Nobody could answer that, except Baby X, who had

just finished its bottle. Baby X's answer was a loud, satisfied burp.

Clearly, nothing at all was wrong. Nevertheless, none of the relatives felt comfortable about buying a present for a Baby X. The cousins who sent the baby a tiny football helmet would not come and visit any more. And the neighbors who sent a pink-flowered romper suit pulled their shades down when the Joneses passed their house.

The *Official Instruction Manual* had warned the new parents that this would happen, so they didn't fret about it. Besides, they were too busy with Baby X and the hundreds of different Xercises for treating it properly.

Ms. and Mr. Jones had to be Xtra careful about how they played with little X. They knew that if they kept bouncing it up in the air and saying how *strong* and *active* it was, they'd be treating it more like a boy than an X. But if all they did was cuddle it and kiss it and tell it how *sweet* and *dainty* it was, they'd be treating it more like a girl than an X.

On page 1,654 of the *Official Instruction Manual*, the scientists prescribed: "plenty of bouncing and plenty of cuddling, *both*. X ought to be strong and sweet and active. Forget about *dainty* altogether."

Meanwhile, the Joneses were worrying about other problems. Toys, for instance. And clothes. On his first shopping trip, Mr. Jones told the store clerk, "I need some clothes and toys for my new baby." The clerk smiled and said, "Well, now, is it a boy or a girl?" "It's an X," Mr.

Jones said, smiling back. But the clerk got all red in the face and said huffily, "In *that* case, I'm afraid I can't help you, sir." So Mr. Jones wandered helplessly up and down the aisles trying to find what X needed. But everything in the store was piled up in sections marked "Boys" or "Girls." There were "Boys' Pajamas" and "Girls' Underwear" and "Boys' Fire Engines" and "Girls' Housekeeping Sets." Mr. Jones went home without buying anything for X. That night he and Ms. Jones consulted page 2,326 of the *Official Instruction Manual.* "Buy plenty of everything!" it said firmly.

So they bought plenty of sturdy blue pajamas in the Boys' Department and cheerful flowered underwear in the Girls' Department. And they bought all kinds of toys. A boy doll that made pee-pee and cried, "Pa-pa." And a girl doll that talked in three languages and said, "I am the Pres-i-dent of Gen-er-al Mo-tors." They also bought a story-book about a brave princess who rescued a handsome prince from his ivory tower, and another one about a sister and brother who grew up to be a baseball star and a ballet star, and you had to guess which was which.

The head scientists of Project Baby X checked all their purchases and told them to keep up the good work. They also reminded the Joneses to see page 4,629 of the *Manual*, where it said, "Never make Baby X feel *embarrassed* or *ashamed* about what it wants to play with. And if X gets dirty climbing rocks, never say 'Nice little Xes don't get dirty climbing rocks.'"

Likewise, it said, "If X falls down and cries, never say 'Brave little Xes don't cry.' Because, of course, nice little Xes *do* get dirty, and brave little Xes *do* cry. No matter how dirty X gets, or how hard it cries, don't worry. It's all part of the Xperiment."

Whenever the Joneses pushed Baby X's stroller in the park, smiling strangers would come over and coo: "Is that a boy or a girl?" The Joneses would smile back and say, "It's an X." The strangers would stop smiling then, and often snarl something nasty—as if the Joneses had snarled at *them*.

By the time X grew big enough to play with other children, the Joneses' troubles had grown bigger, too. Once a little girl grabbed X's shovel in the sandbox, and zonked X on the head with it. "Now, now, Tracy," the little girl's mother began to scold, "little girls mustn't hit little—" and she turned to ask X, "Are you a little boy or a little girl, dear?"

Mr. Jones, who was sitting near the sandbox, held his breath and crossed his fingers.

X smiled politely at the lady, even though X's head had never been zonked so hard in its life. "I'm a little X," X replied.

"You're a *what*?" the lady exclaimed angrily. "You're a little b-r-a-t, you mean!"

"But little girls mustn't hit little Xes, either!" said X, retrieving the shovel with another polite smile. "What good does hitting do, anyway?"

X's father, who was still holding his breath, finally let it out, uncrossed his fingers, and grinned back at X.

And at their next secret Project Baby X meeting, the scientists grinned, too. Baby X was doing fine.

But then it was time for X to start school. The Joneses were really worried about this, because school was even more full of rules for boys and girls, and there were no rules for Xes. The teacher would tell boys to form one line, and girls to form another line. There would be boys' games and girls' games, and boys' secrets and girls' secrets. The school library would have a list of recommended books for girls, and a different list of recommended books for boys. There would even be a bathroom marked BOYS and another one marked GIRLS. Pretty soon boys and girls would hardly talk to each other. What would happen to poor little X?

The Joneses spent weeks consulting their *Instruction Manual* (there were 249½ pages of advice under "First Day of School"), and attending urgent special conferences with the smart scientists of Project Baby X.

The scientists had to make sure that X's mother had taught X how to throw and catch a ball properly, and that X's father had been sure to teach X what to serve at a doll's tea party. X had to know how to shoot marbles and how to jump rope and, most of all, what to say when the Other Children asked whether X was a Boy or Girl.

Finally, X was ready. The Joneses helped X button on a nice new pair of red-and-white checked overalls, and sharpened six pencils for X's nice new pencil box, and marked X's name clearly on all the books in its nice new bookbag. X brushed its teeth and combed its hair, which just about covered its ears, and remembered to put a napkin in its lunchbox.

The Joneses had asked X's teacher if the class could line up alphabetically, instead of forming separate lines for boys and girls. And they had asked if X could use the principal's bathroom, because it wasn't marked anything except BATHROOM. X's teacher promised to take care of all those problems. But nobody could help X with the biggest problem of all—Other Children.

Nobody in X's class had ever known an X before. What would they think? How would X make friends?

You couldn't tell what X was by studying its clothes—overalls don't even button right-to-left, like girls' clothes, or left-to-right, like boys' clothes. And you couldn't guess whether X had a girl's short haircut or a boy's long haircut. And it was very hard to tell by the games X liked to play. Either X played ball very well for a girl, or else X played house very well for a boy.

Some of the children tried to find out by asking X tricky questions, like "Who's your favorite sports star?" That was easy. X had two favorite sports stars: a girl jockey named Robyn Smith and a boy archery champion named Robin Hood. Then they asked, "What's your favorite TV program?" And that was even easier. X's favorite TV program was "Lassie," which stars a girl dog played by a boy dog.

When X said that its favorite toy was a doll, everyone decided that X must be a girl. But then X said that the doll was really a robot, and that X had computerized it; and that it was programmed to bake fudge brownies and then clean up the kitchen. After X told them that, the other children gave up guessing what X was. All they knew was they'd sure like to see X's doll.

After school, X wanted to play with the other children. "How about shooting some baskets in the gym?" X asked the girls. But all they did was make faces and giggle behind X's back.

"How about weaving some baskets in the arts and crafts room?" X asked the boys. But they all made faces and giggled behind X's back, too.

That night, Ms. and Mr. Jones asked X how things had gone at school. X told them sadly that the lessons were okay, but otherwise school was a terrible place for an X. It seemed as if Other Children would never want an X for a friend.

Once more, the Joneses reached for their *Instruction Manual*. Under "Other Children," they found the following message: "What did you Xpect? *Other Children* have to obey all the silly boy-girl rules, because their parents taught them to. Lucky X—you don't have to stick to the rules at all! All you have to do is be yourself. P.S. We're not saying it'll be easy."

X liked being itself. But X cried a lot that night, partly because it felt afraid. So X's father held X tight, and cuddled it, and couldn't help crying a little, too. And X's mother cheered them both up by reading an Xciting story about an enchanted prince called Sleeping Handsome, who woke up when Princess Charming kissed him.

The next morning, they all felt much better, and little X went back to school with a brave smile and a clean pair of red-and-white checked overalls.

There was a seven-letter-word spelling bee in class that day. And a seven-lap boys' relay race in the gym. And a seven-layer-cake baking contest in the girls' kitchen corner. X won the spelling bee. X also won the relay race. And X almost won the baking contest, except it forgot to light the oven. Which only proves that nobody's perfect.

One of the Other Children noticed something else, too. He said: "Winning or losing doesn't seem to count to X. X seems to have fun being good at boys' skills *and* girls' skills."

"Come to think of it," said another one of the Other Children, "maybe X is having twice as much fun as we are!"

So after school that day, the girl who beat X at the baking contest gave X a big slice of her prize-winning cake. And the boy X beat in the relay race asked X to race him home.

From then on, some really funny things began to happen. Susie, who sat next to X in class, suddenly refused to wear pink dresses to school any more. She insisted on wearing red-and-white checked overalls—just like X's.

Overalls, she told her parents, were much better for climbing monkey bars.

Then Jim, the class football nut, started wheeling his little sister's doll carriage around the football field. He'd put on his entire football uniform, except for the helmet. Then he'd put the helmet *in* the carriage, lovingly tucked under an old set of shoulder pads. Then he'd start jogging around the field, pushing the carriage and singing "Rockabye Baby" to his football helmet. He told his family that X did the same thing, so it must be okay. After all, X was now the team's star quarterback.

Susie's parents were horrified by her behavior, and Jim's parents were worried sick about his. But the worst came when the twins, Joe and Peggy, decided to share everything with each other. Peggy used Joe's hockey skates, and his microscope, and took half his newspaper route. Joe used Peggy's needlepoint kit, and her cookbooks, and took two of her three baby-sitting jobs. Peggy started running the lawn mower, and Joe started running the vacuum cleaner.

Their parents weren't one bit pleased with Peggy's wonderful biology experiments, or with Joe's terrific needlepoint pillows. They didn't care that Peggy mowed the lawn better, and that Joe vacuumed the carpet better. In fact they were furious. It's all that little X's fault, they agreed. Just because X doesn't know what it is, or what it's supposed to be, it wants to get everybody *else* mixed up, too!

Peggy and Joe were forbidden to play with X any more.

So was Susie, and then Jim, and then *all* the Other Children. But it was too late; the Other Children stayed mixed up and happy and free, and refused to go back to the way they'd been before X.

Finally, Joe and Peggy's parents decided to call an emergency meeting of the school's Parents' Association, to discuss "The X Problem." They sent a report to the principal stating that X was a "disruptive influence." They demanded immediate action. The Joneses, they said, should be *forced* to tell whether X was a boy or a girl. And then X should be *forced* to behave like whichever it was. If the Joneses refused to tell, the Parents' Association said, then X must take an Xamination. The school psychiatrist must Xamine it physically and mentally, and issue a full report. If X's test showed it was a boy, it would have to obey all the boys' rules. If it proved to be a girl, X would have to obey all the girls' rules.

And if X turned out to be some kind of mixed-up misfit, then X should be Xpelled from the school. Immediately!

The principal was very upset. Disruptive influence? Mixed-up misfit? But X was an Xcellent student. All the teachers said it was a delight to have X in their classes. X was president of the student council. X had won first prize in the talent show, and second prize in the art show, and honorable mention in the science fair, and six athletic events on field day, including the potato race.

Nevertheless, insisted the Parents' Association, X is a

Problem Child. X is the Biggest Problem Child we have ever seen!

So the principal reluctantly notified X's parents that numerous complaints about X's behavior had come to the school's attention. And that after the psychiatrist's Xamination, the school would decide what to do about X.

The Joneses reported this at once to the scientists, who referred them to page 85,759 of the *Instruction Manual.* "Sooner or later," it said, "X will have to be Xamined by a psychiatrist. This may be the only way any of us will know for sure whether X is mixed up—or whether everyone else is."

The night before X was to be Xamined, the Joneses tried not to let X see how worried they were. "What if—?" Mr. Jones would say. And Ms. Jones would reply, "No use worrying." Then a few minutes later, Ms. Jones would say, "What if—?" and Mr. Jones would reply, "No use worrying."

X just smiled at them both, and hugged them hard and didn't say much of anything. X was thinking, What if—? And then X thought: No use worrying.

At Xactly 9 o'clock the next day, X reported to the school psychiatrist's office. The principal, along with a committee from the Parents' Association, X's teacher, X's classmates, and Ms. and Mr. Jones, waited in the hall outside. Nobody knew the details of the tests X was to be given, but everybody knew they'd be *very* hard, and that they'd reveal Xactly what everyone wanted to know about X, but were afraid to ask.

It was terribly quiet in the hall. Almost spooky. Once in a while, they would hear a strange noise inside the room. There were buzzes. And a beep or two. And several bells. An occasional light would flash under the door. The Joneses thought it was a white light, but the principal thought it was blue. Two or three children swore it was either yellow or green. And the Parents' Committee missed it completely.

Through it all, you could hear the psychiatrist's low voice, asking hundreds of questions, and X's higher voice, answering hundreds of answers.

The whole thing took so long that everyone knew it must be the most complete Xamination anyone had ever had to take. Poor X, the Joneses thought. Serves X right, the Parents' Committee thought. I wouldn't like to be in X's overalls right now, the children thought.

At last, the door opened. Everyone crowded around to hear the results. X didn't look any different; in fact, X was smiling. But the psychiatrist looked terrible. He looked as if he was crying! "What happened?" everyone began shouting. Had X done something disgraceful? "I wouldn't be a bit surprised!" muttered Peggy and Joe's parents. "Did X flunk the *whole* test?" cried Susie's parents. "Or just the most important part?" yelled Jim's parents.

"Oh, dear," sighed Mr. Jones.

"Oh, dear," sighed Ms. Jones.

"*Sssh*," ssshed the principal. "The psychiatrist is trying to speak."

Wiping his eyes and clearing his throat, the psychiatrist began, in a hoarse whisper. "In my opinion," he whispered—you could tell he must be very upset—"in my opinion, young X here—"

"Yes? Yes?" shouted a parent impatiently.

"*Sssh!*" ssshed the principal.

"Young *Sssh* here, I mean young X," said the doctor, frowning, "is just about—"

"Just about *what*? Let's have it!" shouted another parent.

". . . just about the *least* mixed-up child I've ever Xamined!" said the psychiatrist.

"Yay for X!" yelled one of the children. And then the others began yelling, too. Clapping and cheering and jumping up and down.

"*SSSH!*" SSShed the principal, but nobody did.

The Parents' Committee was angry and bewildered. How *could* X have passed the whole Xamination? Didn't X have an *identity* problem? Wasn't X mixed up at *all*? Wasn't X any kind of a misfit? How could it *not* be, when it didn't even *know* what it was? And why was the psychiatrist crying?

Actually, he had stopped crying and was smiling politely through his tears. "Don't you see?" he said. "I'm crying because it's wonderful! X has absolutely no identity problem! X isn't one bit mixed up! As for being a misfit—

ridiculous! X knows perfectly well what it is! Don't you, X?" The doctor winked. X winked back.

"But what *is* X?" shrieked Peggy and Joe's parents. "*We* still want to know what it is!"

"Ah, yes," said the doctor, winking again. "Well, don't worry. You'll all know one of these days. And you won't need me to tell you."

"Well? What does he mean?" some of the parents grumbled suspiciously.

Susie and Peggy and Joe all answered at once. "He means that by the time X's sex matters, it won't be a secret any more!"

With that, the doctor began to push through the crowd toward X's parents. "How do you do," he said, somewhat stiffly. And then he reached out to hug them both. "If I ever have an X of my own," he whispered, "I sure hope you'll lend me your instruction manual."

Needless to say, the Joneses were very happy. The Project Baby X scientists were rather pleased, too. So were Susie, Jim, Peggy, Joe, and all the Other Children. The Parents' Association wasn't, but they had promised to accept the psychiatrist's report, and not make any more trouble. They even invited Ms. and Mr. Jones to become honorary members, which they did.

Later that day, all X's friends put on their red-and-white checked overalls and went over to see X. They found X in the back yard, playing with a very tiny baby that none of them had ever seen before. The baby was wearing very tiny red-and-white overalls.

"How do you like our new baby?" X asked the Other Children proudly.

"It's got cute dimples," said Jim.

"It's got husky biceps, too," said Susie.

"What kind of baby is it?" asked Joe and Peggy.

X frowned at them. "Can't you tell?" Then X broke into a big, mischievous grin. *"It's a Y!"*

SUGGESTED READING

OTHER BOOKS AND JOURNALS YOU CAN READ TO HELP YOU BETTER UNDERSTAND PREJUDICE

City Kids Speak by City Kids (Random House, New York, New York, 1994). Using photos, cartoons, interviews, essays, and testimonials, the book provides examples of how young people live with and struggle to overcome prejudice.

Family: A Portrait of Gay and Lesbian America by Nancy Andrews (HarperCollins, San Francisco, California, 1994). Using her skills and experience as a staff photographer for the *Washington Post*, Andrews's collection of interviews and stories, illustrated with black-and-white photographs, challenges many of the stereotypes about gays and lesbians.

Freedom's Children: Young Civil Rights Activists Tell Their Own Stories by Ellen Levine (Putnam, New York, New York, 1993). Thirty-two African Americans reflect on how their actions changed America.

Is It a Choice? Answers to Three Hundred of the Most Frequently Asked Questions About Gay Men and Lesbians by Eric Marcus (HarperCollins, San Francisco, California, 1993). For homosexuals and heterosexuals, this handy reference answers a range of questions about gender identity, coming out, and living in a homophobic world.

It's Our World Too! Stories of Young People Making a Difference by Phillip Hoose (Little, Brown, Boston, Masssachusetts, 1993). Courageous young people tell their own stories about how they worked to change their lives, schools, neighborhoods, cities, and the world. The book also provides tactics and strategies you can use to bring about change.

The Race Mixer by Communities Against Hate (Communities Against Hate, Eugene, Oregon, 1994). A bimonthly newsletter dedicated to preserving civil rights for all regardless of race, gender, sexual orientation, religion, or economic status.

Respecting Our Differences: A Guide to Getting Along in a Changing World by Lynn Duvall (Free Spirit, Minneapolis, Minnesota, 1994). Young people from across the country talk about how they are unlearning prejudice in their schools and communities. The guide also helps young people examine attitudes, stereotypes, and prejudices while focusing on learning to become more accepting and understanding of those outside of one's cultural, ethnic, or gender group.

Speaking Out: Teenagers Take on Race, Sex, and Identity by Susan Kuklin (Putnam, New York, New York, 1993). Young people address the issues of gender, race, class, sexual orientation, and stature.

Spreading Poison: A Book About Racism and Prejudice by John Langone (Little, Brown, Boston, Massachusetts, 1993). Along with the contributions of various racial and ethnic groups in the United States, this book examines how racial, gender, and religious discrimination have established a disturbing tone and tenor in our lives.

Still a Nation of Immigrants by Brent Ashbranner (Cobblehill Books/Dutton, New York, New York, 1993). Who are today's immigrants? What contributions have they made? What impact is immigration having on the nation? Ashbranner examines the important roles that immigrants have played in making this nation a multicultural, multiethnic society.

The White Power Movement: America's Racist Hate Groups by Elaine Landau (Millbrook Press, Brookfield, Connecticut, 1994). The history of the Ku Klux Klan, the White Aryan Resistance, and the Identity Church are discussed in this book, along with the work of antiprejudice and civil rights organizations, including the Anti-Defamation League of B'nai B'rith, the NAACP, and the Southern Poverty Law Center.

OTHER HELPFUL RESOURCES

Against Borders: Promoting Books for a Multicultural World by Hazel Rochman (American Library Association/Booklist Publications, Chicago, Illinois, 1993). This comprehensive, annotated bibliography directs the reader to books that challenge the indignities of racism, sexism, anti-Semitism, homophobia, and classism. It also provides some excellent cross-cultural titles.

Books Without Bias: A Guide to Evaluating Children's Literature for Handicapism by Beverly Slapin (Squeaky Wheel Press, Berkeley, California, 1987). A guide to some of the best books about disabilities for young children and adolescents.

ALSO OF INTEREST

Class 2000: The Prejudice Puzzle by National Public Radio Outreach (National Public Radio, Washington, D.C., 1994) examines the effects of prejudice on young people today by interviewing several of its victims. Geared for grades six and up, the series includes an academically gifted black teenager whose aggressive manner caused him to be barred from public school, children at a "fat camp," and a high school champion athlete who is a little person. The three half-hour cassettes come with a teaching guide.

About the Contributors

Fran Arrick, Judy Angel, and Maggie Twohill are pseudonyms of the same author. She has written many middle grade and young adult novels, including *God's Radar*; *Nice Girl from Good Home*; *Yours Truly*; and most recently, *What You Don't Know Can Kill You*, a novel about teenagers and AIDS.

Lynda Barry (b. 1956) was born in Seattle, Washington. She is a novelist, playwright, recording artist, and nationally syndicated cartoonist whose books include *Come Over, Come Over*; *Down the Street*; *Everything in the World; Girls Boys*; *The Fun House*; and most recently *It's So Magic*. She is also the recipient of the Joe A. Calloway Playwriting Award.

Julie Blackwomon (b. 1943) is a self-described feminist. A mother and a grandmother, she lives and works in Philadelphia, Pennsylvania. Her fiction is featured in *Voyages Out 2* and her poetry in *Revolutionary Blues and Other Fevers*. Most recently she has been published in *Woman's Glib*, *She Who Is Lost Is Remembered*, and *The Parenting Anthology*. She is currently working on a novel.

Sandra Cisneros (b. 1954) was born in Chicago, Illinois. In 1985 she won the American Book Award from the Before Columbus Foundation for her novel *The House on Mango Street*. She is the author of a short story collection, *Women Hollering Creek*; two books of poetry, *My Wicked Wicked Ways* and *Loose Woman*; as well as a children's book, *Hairs/Pelitas*. *Carmelo* is her most recent novel.

Chris Crutcher (b. 1946) was raised in Cascade, Idaho, and currently lives in Spokane, Washington. He is the author of four young adult novels: *Chinese Handcuffs*; *The Crazy Horse Electric Game*; *Stotan!*; and *Running Loose*, all of which were named ALA Best Books for Young Adults, as well as the short story collection *Athletic Shorts*, an ALA Best Book for Young Adults and an ALA Recommended Book for Reluctant Young Readers.

Jack Forbes (b. 1934) was born in Long Beach, California, and is of Powahatan-Delaware ancestry. He is the chair of Native American studies at the University of California at Davis and the author of several books, including *Columbus and Other Cannibals* and *Blacks and Native Americans*. His articles often appear in *The Journal of Ethnic Studies*. *Only Approved Indians: A Collection of Short Stories* is his most recent book.

Lois Gould (b. 1946) was born in the Bronx, New York, and is a novelist, journalist, and essayist. She has written for several national publications, including the *New York Times*. She is also the author of the novel *Such Good Friends* and *Q: A Perfect Child's Story*.

Mavis Hara (b. 1949) was born in Honolulu, Hawaii. Her fiction has appeared in literary journals as well as in numerous anthologies, including *Bamboo Ridge* and *Growing Up Asian American*.

Denise Sherer Jacobson (b. 1950) was born in the Bronx, New York. Her articles, reviews, and short stories have appeared in newspapers and anthologies, including the *San Francisco Chronicle* and *Across the Generations*. Ms. Jacobson recently completed her first novel, *A Question of David*.

Marie G. Lee (b. 1964) was born in Hibbing, Minnesota, and published her first short story at age sixteen in *Seventeen* magazine. She has written numerous articles and three young adult novels: *Finding My Voice*, a 1993 ALA Best Book for Reluctant Young Readers and recipient of the 1993 Friends of the American Writer Award; *If it Hadn't Been for Yoon Jun*; and *Saying Good-bye.*

Flannery O'Connor (1925–64) was born in Savannah, Georgia, and died at the age of 39. During her short life, she came to be regarded as one of America's foremost writers. She twice won the O. Henry short story award, once in 1956 and again in 1963; published two novels, *Wise Blood* and *The Violent Bear It Away*; and two collections of short stories, *A Good Man Is Hard to Find* and *Everything that Rises Must Converge.* Although she espoused racial equality in her fiction, recent private correspondence has come to light that seems to contradict her public stand. However, the full import of her letters to long-time friend Maryat Lee has not been fully examined.

Mitali Perkins (b. 1963) was born in Calcutta, India, and from there moved with her family to Cameroon, Ghana, England, Mexico, and New York City before finally settling in the San Francisco Bay area. *The Sunita Experiment* is her first novel for young adults.

Ntozake Shange (b. 1948) was born Paulette Williams in Trenton, New Jersey. In 1971, she adopted a Zulu name to protest her Western roots. It means "she who comes with her own things" and "she who walks like a lion." Her work *For Colored Girls who have considered suicide / when the rainbow* *is enuf* was produced on Broadway in 1975 and received an Obie. *Liliane: Resurrection of the Daughter* is her most recent novel.

Kate Walker (b. 1950) was born in New South Wales, Australia, where she currently resides. Ms. Walker has written a number of children's picture books, and her work has been published in magazines and anthologies. Her first young adult novel, *Peter*, received the 1991 Australian Human Rights Award and was named by the ALA a 1994 Best Book for Young Adults, a 1994 Notable Children's Book, and a 1994 Recommended Book for Reluctant Young Readers.

Jacqueline Woodson (b. 1963) was born in Ohio and grew up in Greenville, South Carolina, and Brooklyn, New York. She is the author of *Last Summer with Maizon*, *Maizon at Blue Hill*, and *Between Madison and Palmetto*, as well as *The Dear One* and *I Hadn't Meant to Tell You This*. Ms. Woodson is also a recipient of the Kenyon Review Award for Literary Excellence in Fiction.

About the Editor

Daphne Muse was born in Washington, D.C., and now lives in Oakland, California. She has coauthored two children's books, including *Children of Africa*. Ms. Muse served on the faculty of the English department of Mills College for ten years, where she taught both writing and multicultural children's literature. For six years she served as the editor and publisher of the *Children's Advocate* newspaper. Her articles appear in the *Washington Post*, the *Black Review of Books*, the *San Francisco Chronicle*, and the *Hungry Mind Review*. Since 1969, Ms. Muse has been a multicultural curriculum consultant and workshop leader for school districts throughout the United States. She has also served as an educational consultant for the Child Development Division of the California State Department of Education and for the Hitachi Foundation. Through workshops for teenagers, her own writing, and the sharing of stories like these, she has gained invaluable insight into experiences young people have with prejudice.

THE EDITOR AND PUBLISHER GRATEFULLY ACKNOWLEDGE THE FOLLOWING FOR GRANTING US PERMISSION TO INCLUDE THEIR STORIES:

- "White Trash" from *The Good Times Are Killing Me* by Lynda Barry. Copyright © 1988 by Lynda Barry. First HarperPerennial edition published 1992. Reprinted by permission of The Real Comet Press, Seattle, WA.
- From *Chernowitz!* by Fran Arrick. Copyright © 1981 by Fran Arrick. Reprinted with the permission of Macmillan Books for Young Readers, an imprint of Simon & Schuster Children's Publishing Division.
- "Only Approved Indians Can Play: Made in USA" by Jack Forbes. Copyright © 1983 by Jack D. Forbes. This story first appeared in *Earth Power Coming: Short Fiction in Native American Literature*, Simon Oritz, editor (Navajo Community College Press, 1983). *Only Approved Indians*, a new collection of Jack Forbes's short stories, will be published in 1995 by the University of Oklahoma Press.
- "Carnival Queen" copyright © 1991 by Mavis Hara. "Carnival Queen" was first published in *Sister Stew*, edited by Juliet S. Kono and Kathy Song (Bamboo Ridge Press, 1991). It was also published in *Growing Up Asian American: An Anthology*, edited by Maria Hong (New York: William Morrow, 1993). Permission to reprint courtesy of Mavis Hara.
- "A Rice Sandwich" from *The House on Mango Street* by Sandra Cisneros. Copyright © 1984 by Sandra Cisneros. Published in the United States by Vintage Books, a division of Random House, Inc., New York, and in hardcover by Alfred A. Knopf in 1994. Reprinted by permission of Susan Bergholz Literary Services, New York.
- "So's Your Mama," by Julie Blackwomon. Copyright © 1981 by Julie Blackwomon. From *Voyages Out 2*, (Seal Press, 1990). First published in *Lesbian Fiction*, Elly Bulkin, editor, (Persephone Press, 1981). Permission to reprint courtesy of Julie Blackwomon.
- "American Bandstand" by Denise Sherer Jacobson. Copyright © 1989 by Denise Sherer Jacobson. First published in *Sinister Wisdom* 39 (Winter 1989–90). Reprinted by permission of Denise Sherer Jacobson.
- From *The Sunita Experiment* by Mitali Perkins. Copyright © 1993 by Mitali Perkins. Reprinted by courtesy of Little, Brown and Company.
- From *Peter* by Kate Walker. Copyright © 1991 by Kate Walker. Reprinted by permission of Houghton Mifflin Co. All rights reserved.
- From *Finding My Voice* by Marie G. Lee. Copyright © 1992 by Marie G. Lee. Reprinted by permission of Houghton Mifflin Co. All rights reserved.
- "Revelation" from *The Complete Stories* by Flannery O'Connor. Copyright © 1964, 1965, 1971 by the Estate of Mary Flannery O'Connor. Reprinted by permission of Farrar, Straus & Giroux, Inc.
- From *Maizon at Blue Hill* by Jacqueline Woodson. Copyright © 1992 by Jacqueline Woodson. Used by permission of Dell Books, a division of Bantam Doubleday Dell Publishing Group, Inc.
- From *Betsey Brown* by Ntozake Shange, copyright © 1985 by Ntozake Shange. Reprinted courtesy of St. Martin's Press.
- "A Brief Moment in the Life of Angus Bethune" from *Athletic Shorts* by Chris Crutcher. Copyright © 1991 by Chris Crutcher. Reprinted by permission of Greenwillow Books, a division of William Morrow & Company, Inc.
- "X: A Fabulous Child's Story" by Lois Gould. Copyright © 1978 by Lois Gould. Reprinted by permission of the Charlotte Sheedy Literary Agency.